SANCTUARY 2

Paul Ashlin

Café Companion Publishing

Published by Cafe Companion

Also by Paul Ashlin
The Education of a Cab Driver
Sanctuary
Coming Soon, Losing Grip

Book Cover Designed by Paul Ashlin
You can contact the author @ paulashlin.com

Previously from Sanctuary
Operation Bird Nest

Fred passes the hostel for the third time; he's familiarizing himself with the area. As he drives this area of Chicago, he considers possible places to carry out his impromptu mission. *Looks like there's a good view from the parking garage. That might just work.* He circles around, searching for the garage entrance.

He presses the large button—a ticket spits out. Snatching the ticket, the mechanical arm swings up. Needing to elevate to get a bird's eye view, he motors up the levels. Making it to the 5th level, he trolls the parking situation—it's at capacity. He gives the 7th level a try, and there are lots of free spaces. Parking, he pauses, whipping his head in both directions. Confident he's alone, he exits the car, moving to the edge. *This looks good. There's a clear view of the hostel and the bus station.* He checks again for anyone watching—he's alone. Drawing a small pair of binos, he peers down, assessing the difficulty of the shot. *Shit, this will be a turkey shoot—not that I've ever been to a turkey shoot.* He chuckles while sliding the binos back into his pocket. Swiveling his head, he checks again—he's still alone. *I think I need something better. It would be too easy for someone to walk up on me.* He decides to walk the street.

Standing on the corner, he studies the patterns. *Huh, I'd thought it would be busier—this is Chicago after all.* Most of the action happens around the bus station. He needs a nest. Surveying the rooftops, he searches. *C'mon, there has to be a good spot around somewhere.* He flashes back to his Vietnam days when he was twenty, doing special ops missions. *This is different. But it's also the same.* He spots a Peet's coffee next to the bus station. *That's it. I'll bet he'll get coffee. That is if he's actually here. I hope your intel is good, Tom. Now, a place to shoot from.*

Crossing the street, he twists around, scanning the roof lines. Most of the buildings are too tall. His eyes return to the garage. *It would be too risky to shoot from where I parked.* He spots it—above the elevator—a perfect nest. *There we go.* There are two, one on the corner of the building and one in the middle of the structure. *It would be too easy to be spotted on the corner, but maybe the middle one. Yeah, that might be the ticket. Now, can I get up there?*

Back in the parking garage, he takes the elevator to the eighth level. Stepping out of the elevator, his head cranes up—it's open to the sky. *Where are the cars? People probably don't want to deal with the snow up here. This might do in a pinch.* He moves to the edge. *Yep, the hostel, the bus station, and Peet's are all in sight. How crazy would that be, Pete gunned down at Peet's.* He chuckles.

Checking the elevator, there's a ladder going to the top. *Crap.* There are metal bars with a lock. He mutters, "Damn, I didn't bring my bolt cutters." Twisting a hundred and eighty degrees, there's a stairway a hundred feet away. *Maybe there?*

He enters, eyes down the stairs, listening. Hearing no footsteps echoing off the walls, he whips his head to the ladder that leads to a hatch. *No lock, maybe it's open?* Climbing the ladder, he gives a slight push—it gives. He pushes open the hatch. Pulling himself through, he stands, gazing at a small ten-by-ten space trashed beer bottles, cans and fast-food wrappers. *Looks like the kids use this as a partying spot. That's probably why the lock is gone.* He eases the hatch close.

The walls are four feet high. He moves to the edge. *Oh my God, this is too perfect.* The hostel, the bus station, and Peet's are all in view. The wall is an ideal height to rest a rifle. He peers through his binos, tracking what he thinks Pete's path will be to get his morning cup of joe. *God, this is perfect.* Surveying the tall buildings in the area, there are two that are the most concerning. *Damn, I can be spotted from both those buildings. Oh well, I'll just have to take that chance.*

Billy nurses his beer. He can't believe his luck finding a bar and grill across the street from the hostel; he has a window seat with a perfect view. Pete checked in hours ago. Billy was happy to get out of his truck after tracking that piss-yellow Caddy all the way from Texas.

Pete emerges. Billy is ready to pounce, but Pete crosses the street, heading his way; Billy eases back into his chair. Pete enters, shaking off the cold, eyeing a row of bistro tables. His eyes lock on Billy—they share a look. Pete sits two tables away; he sits with his back to Billy. Billy orders another beer. The waiter stops at Pete's table, handing him a menu.

Pete says, "Thank you. Ahh, excuse me." The waiter stops. "Is there a bank around here?"

"A bank?"

"Yeah, something within walking distance."

"Ahhh . . . yeah, I think there's one down on West Adams." The waiter points. "That way. It's about nine blocks or so. It's a nice walk if it's not too cold."

"Okay, thanks. Oh, and I was reading, there's a bus station around here?"

"Yeah, that's two blocks away. Up the street, take a right. It's real close."

"Okay. Thanks." Pete digs into the menu.

Billy digests the information. *Bank and bus station? I don't think he's staying long.*

Billy's float is giving emergency signals, he's needed to pee for the last forty minutes; it's getting painful, but he's not letting Pete slip away. Finishing, Pete is on the move, slipping out to the sidewalk. He pauses before starting to his right. Billy follows. *Thank God.* Walking helps him hang on a little longer. *Shit, I'm going to need a bathroom soon.*

At the corner, Pete turns right, seeing the sign for the bus station. *Damn, this is close,* Pete thinks. Walking into the bus terminal, he plants himself in the middle of the lobby, studying the departure board. Billy keeps close enough to eavesdrop. Pete bellies up to the ticket counter.

"Hi sir, how can I help you?"

"Yeah, howdy, I'm wondering if you have regular trips to Milwaukee?" Pete asks.

"Yep. Three times a day. We have a 6:45 am, 1:00 pm, and the last bus of the day is 9:45. They're all twenty dollars. Do you want a ticket?"

"Not yet. I have a few things I need to do. I'll be back. Thanks."

"Uh-huh," the clerk replies.

Billy can't take it, bolting for the restroom. Pete glances at the big clock on the wall, before heading back outside.

Billy stands at the urinal, letting the floodgates open. *God, that feels good. Okay, so this dude is going to Milwaukee. The question is, when?*

Planting himself on the sidewalk, Pete takes in the surroundings. *Shit, look at that, a Peet's. Sweet.* He gets a closer look.

Back on the street corner, Fred spots the Bar and Grill across the street from the hostel. *Okay, let's see if this asshole is here.* Walking to the front of the Bar and Grill, he notices all the tables lining the window. *Damn, this is like a dream.* He settles at a table, ordering a burger and beer—he watches.

The waiter makes his third pass. Fred gives in, ordering another beer. Before the beer arrives, he spots Pete crossing the street, heading to the hostel. *There you are, asshole.* Fred glances at his watch. *I don't know what your source is Tom, but they're right on target. I'll bet the asshole is settling in for the evening.* The beer arrives. Fred raises his glass. *Here's to you, asshole.*

Billy follows Pete into the hostel, inquiring about a room.

"I think we have one," the clerk says. "Yes, we have two. Would you like one?"

"Yeah."

"Okay, I need you to sign in, and that will be fifty dollars."

It's a chilly morning. Up early, Fred wants to validate his theory that Pete will make a run to get coffee in the morning. He grabs a spot by the door. He waits, sipping his cup of joe. Pete enters, ordering a black coffee. *Bingo.* Fred notes the time. Billy enters. Pete sits at the table next to Fred, watching Billy order.

Pete wonders, hearing the southern drawl. *Is that a southern boy?* Billy waits for his drink, and Pete approaches. "Hey, excuse me? Y'all from down south?" Pete asks.

"Huh?" Billy faces Pete. "If ya call being from Texas, the south."

"Funny. So, you're from Texas?"

"Yeah."

"So am I."

"Really? What part?"

"Ahh, it's a small town ya never heard of."

"Huh, me too."

"Whatcha doin' here?"

"I'm in town for a conference."

"Huh, me too."

"Small world."

"Isn't it? I'm William."

"I'm Ted," Pete says. They shake.

"I got to go. Maybe I'll see you around."

"Maybe. Nice to meet ya."

"Same here," Billy grabs his drink, ducking out the door.

Fred Ponders, *Huh, what are the odds two Texas boys would meet at this Peet's?*

With his plan in place, Fred climbs the ladder, lugging his guitar case. The morning is the same as yesterday; it's cold but clear, with very little wind. Fred opens the guitar case, pulling out the rifle parts. He assembles the gun, loads it, and sets it aside. He gazes through his binos, running through Pete's path to Peet's.

He'll come out, probably pause. If the traffic is light, he'll probably cross in the middle of the street. If there's traffic, he'll go up to the corner, crossing at the light. Tracking the path, he considers the place to make the shot. *I might hit someone else if I shoot him at the coffee shop. If I shoot him in front of the bus station, it'll be too easy to track the shot. Yeah, the best place is if he crosses the street or at the crosswalk. He'll be coming toward me. Yeah, that's the best place.*

Fred locks on Billy coming out of the hostel. *Isn't that the kid from Peet's?* Billy pauses before heading to the corner. Fred tracks him. *Now, don't get distracted.*

Fred glances at his watch. *Okay, showtime, if this guy is a creature of habit.* Fred readies his gun. Pete pops out of the hostel, pausing in between two parked cars, whipping his head in both directions. A car passes. Another vehicle follows, but Pete calculates he can slip through and darts into the street. Fred squeezes the trigger. The gunshot cracks the morning air, echoing off the buildings, making it hard to pinpoint the origin of the shot. The shot strikes Pete's chest, slicing through his body above his heart—stopping his momentum. A truck strikes him. The sound of meat slapping against metal and cracking bones grabs the attention of those close by. The impact crushes the side of Pete's body, launching him airborne. He lands on the hood of a parked car like a sack of potatoes, before slithering off the hood, landing in between two parked cars. He flounders on his back, looking like a fish out of water, gasping for air.

"What the . . .?" Fred mutters, moving the gun out of sight. The truck blocks his view of Pete. Locking his binos on the truck, he can't tell who's driving.

In one frantic motion, Billy pops out of his truck, racing to Pete's resting place. Billy pops up, screaming, "Oh, my God! He just ran in front of me."

"You've gotta be kidding," Fred mumbles. "Shit, it's the kid from Peet's." Fred breaks his rifle down, collects the spent casing, and scrambles out of the nest. He places the case in the trunk and drives to the exit with incredible efficiency.

Billy bends over, whispering in Pete's ear. Pete gasps for his final breath.

"That's for Little John, ya piece of shit."

Confusion registers on Pete's face. It is interesting when you watch someone die. First there's life, and then they slip into nothingness as their eyes go dead, lifeless.

Billy pops up. "Oh, my God, oh, my God. He ran in front of me. He ran in front of me."

A policeman on foot responds to the scene. "What happened?" Trevor asks.

Billy faces him. "He ran in front of me."

"Let me in there," Trevor says. Billy backs up. Trevor examines Pete, checking for a pulse—nothing. The streak of blood on the car hood catches his eye. "What happened?"

"I was driving, and he popped out," Billy says. "I couldn't stop."

The cop gazes back at Pete, lying in a pool of blood. The cop talks into the mic mounted on his shoulder as he circles Billy's truck.

"Looks like we got a pedestrian all broken up. Appears to be a casualty, male, at . . ." Trevor searches for the address. "310 Halsted Street. And send the lab boys."

"How bad is he?"

"Bad."

"Is he dead?"

"I think so? But I'm dealing with a lot of stuff. I'm alone."

"Okay, they're on their way."

"Oh, my God. Oh, my God," Billy repeats.

"Okay, calm down, calm down," the cop says. "Tell me again, what happened?"

It was two blocks to the freeway. Fred drives, thinking, *Man, the nest couldn't have been in any better of a spot.* Approaching East Chicago and Wolf Lake, he takes the off-ramp. The lake is to the left, and so is the Lost Marsh Golf Course. He follows the signs, looking for a place close to the lake. The road winds—a parking lot appears. The lot is empty; there are a few cars covered in snow. *Looks like the snow has killed business.* He parks at the lake's edge. *Man, this is great.*

Cautious, Fred surveys the area for prying eyes—no one is in sight. Opening the trunk, he grabs the handle to the guitar case, scooting it into position. Opening the case, he picks out the barrel. He wipes it down, and slides it up his sleeve. He picks his spot. *There, between those trees.* Stationing himself between two large trees on the edge of the lake, sling the barrel into the lake—splash. He waits—watching. Confident no one has seen him, he returns to his car.

Billy watches the emergency crews work on Pete. A photographer takes pictures of the scene. They've blocked off the street, which is buzzing like beehive with lookie-loos, the police, and the forensic team.

"Hey, Trevor," Noah calls out. Trevor is interviewing a witness.

"Just a sec," Trevor replies, raising his finger. "Okay, thank you," he says to the witness. Trevor dashes over to Noah.

In a low voice, Noah says, "Hey man, this guy was shot."

Trevor narrows his eyes, peering down at Jeremy, who's bent over Pete's body, nodding.

Trevor tilts his head. "What are you guys talking about?"

Noah points. "Right here below his throat,"

Trevor inspects the wound. "Jesus, now we gotta shooter?"

"It sure looks like it," Jeremy replies.

"Damn."

"There's a bullet around here somewhere," Noah says.

"How do you know that?" Trevor asks.

"It looks like it exited out of his right kidney," Noah replies.

"But you said he was shot below the throat?"

"The bullet probably tumbled through his body."

"Damn. I knew there was something weird about this. Okay, thanks." Trevor pops up, focusing on Billy's truck. "Mr. Bates."

"Yeah."

"Can you come over here?"

"Sure." Billy joins Trevor.

"Okay, so he pops out into the street before you could stop—"

"Right."

"So, was he looking at you?"

"No, I think I hit him on his side. He was looking that way." Billy points.

"Do you have any guns in the truck?"

"What?"

"Guns, do you have any guns?"

"Ahh . . . yeah, I have a pistol in the glove box."

"Okay, don't move. I am going to retrieve it. Is that okay with you?"

"Ahh, sure," Billy replies. *What the hell does this guy want with my gun?*

Trevor waves over a forensics person. "Have you got an evidence bag?"

Evidence bag? Billy wonders. *Oh shit, this isn't good.*

Trevor, in a low voice, "Hey, comb the area for bullets."

"What?"

"Yeah. Start over by where the body landed."

"Okay."

Fred sees a truck stop up ahead. Time for fuel. Pulling next to the pump, he goes inside to pay with cash. There's a payphone off to the side. He returns to the car and refuels. As the gas pumps, he opens the trunk and then the case, picking out the gunstock. While wiping it down, he surveys who might be watching. *There's a camera somewhere. I just know it.* Preparing for this situation, he's brought a newspaper. Wrapping the gunstock in a few pages, he drops it in the trash.

He tops off the gas and pulls the car to the side, parking. He goes back inside.

"Hello," Tom answers.

"Tom. It's Fred."

"Oh my God, are you okay?"

"Yeah, yeah, I'm fine. I'm back on the road again. Any update?"

"Oh, I'm so glad you called. Head home. Kathy's strong enough, they're going to transport her to a Cleveland hospital."

"That's good news."

"Yeah, we can get out of here. We'll meet you at the house."

"Okay, excellent. I'll see you at home."

"Hey, Fred."

"Yeah."

"That must have been some part?"

"It sure was."

They place Billy in the back of a police car.

"Am I being arrested?" Billy asks.

"No, no. This is just a better place, you know, while we sort things out," Trevor replies.

"What are ya sorting out?"

Trevor leans in, whispering, "The man you hit was shot."

"What?"

"Yeah, crazy, I know. So, do you have any problem waiting here?"

"No."

"Okay, good. Thank you for your cooperation." Trevor closes the door. Trevor makes his way back to Pete. Rod, from the forensic team, examines Pete. "So, have you got anything?"

Rod pops up; he likes to talk with his hands. "With his body being thrown so far by the truck, it's making this hard. The driver didn't hit his brakes until well after he struck him."

"Yeah, he said he just popped out on him."

"Looking at the skid marks." He points. "I'd say he was traveling somewhere between forty-five or fifty when he struck him." He points at Pete. "That's why the body ended up between the cars."

"What about the gunshot?'

"Hard to say, because the body traveled so far, but I looked at the blood on the hood of the car and how he landed. I think he was shot just before he was hit by the truck."

"Damn."

"I know. Who is this guy? Is this a mob thing?"

"Shit, I don't know? I don't think so?" Trevor replies. "You want to hear something that will really cook your noodle?"

"Sure."

"They're both from Texas."

"What? A grudge thing?"

"Maybe. I am trying to find out if they knew each other. So, is there a third party?"

"Looking at the entrance wound, I don't see how the driver would have shot him, but I wouldn't rule it out yet. We need an autopsy."

"Yeah, I know. The captain is going to love this shit. Christ—"

"What?" Rod asks.

Trevor pulls out his notebook, flipping through the pages. "Yep, here it is. This old woman I interviewed said she heard a car backfire. Shit. Looks like we got a shooter."

"You think the driver and the shooter were working together?"

"Isn't that a great question?" Trevor scans the buildings, locking on the garage. "Damn, who is this guy?"

"Actually, it's who *was* this guy?"

"Right," Trevor speaks into his mic. "Hey, tell the captain it looks like we have a shooter."

"Oh, Trevor, the captain is going to love you."

Sanctuary II

That's the thing about fate; it places you where you're supposed to be.

One
Julian

Julian leans over the pictures of the murder scene, spreading them out, combing over them for the seventeenth time. *What am I missing?* He pinches the bridge of his nose, rubbing his eyes. *Why am I doing this? Why can't I let this go? Christ, I don't even know what I'm looking for. Perez is right—I'm a mental case. What do I care about a Texas boy running over another Texas boy?* Stroking his chin, he rocks back in his chair. *One shot. Who only needs one shot? An assassin. Yeah, an assassin. Why would an assassin gun down this guy from Texas—in Chicago?* Julian closes his eyes, swiveling the chair, getting in a rhythm. *Shot. Ran over. Or ran over and then shot—what's the difference? He's dead.* He stops. His eyes pop open—an insight—a revelation. The thought evaporates. *Damn.*

He stands, stretching his shoulders and arching his back. He glances at his watch. *I've been doing this too long. I need a break.* He paces. *Wait a second. Were the driver and the shooter working together?* The insight reinvigorates him. He slaps his ass back into the chair. *Damn, why didn't I think of that before? Wow, is that it?* He rummages through the file. *Let's say that's true. That would have been a helluva thing to coordinate.* Julian picks up the photo of Pete's final resting spot, studying it. *If it's true, the shooter must also be from Texas.* He talks to the photo like it will answer. "Why are these Texas people settling their shit in Chicago?" His newfound enthusiasm fades; he slumps, flicking the photo back to the file like he's trying to toss a playing card into a hat.

He focuses on the shooter. *This shooter is a pro. Shit, am I dealing with a secret underground society? Let's say this coach pissed off somebody, so they got rid of him. Who did he piss off? He did use that family down in Mooresville for target practice. I'm sure they wanted him dead. Maybe they made a call? Even if they did, how did they know he was in Chicago?*

He sits up, laser locking on the baggy—the one with the bullet. Lifting the baggy to the light, he snatches the bullet from the bag. Palming the bullet, he closes his eyes, meditating like the bullet will speak, giving up its secrets. It's the only real evidence, and it's useless. He checks the notes. *Three people—three people heard a car backfire.* He returns the bullet to the baggy. As frustrating as this case is, it's also intriguing. He decides to return to the crime scene—again.

Pacing in front of the hostel, Julian gazes at Pete's final landing spot. He stops, considering Pete's final movements. He twists toward the front door of the hostel. *He pops out of the hostel, moving to the edge of the sidewalk. He waits, picking out his spot to make his move. He bolts into the street, thinking he can cross before the truck hits him. Yeah, he probably thought he was fast enough to do that. But then—smack—a bullet to the chest. Yeah, a bullet to the chest will slow your ass down. The truck mows his ass down.* He freezes—a jolt pulses through his body—an insight. *Were the driver and the shooter working together? Damn. What if that was true?* He rubs his chin, cupping his mouth.

Julian flips his approach; he's done this before, but why not give it another try? *If I was going to kill this guy, how would I do it? What would I need to know to be able to pull it off? Man, with two people, this gets a lot more complicated. How did they track him? That's the question, isn't it? Damn, this was so well executed.* He's getting distracted—again.

If I were going to shoot him. His eyes lift, scanning the buildings, looking for a nest. *I'd need a place to shoot from. It had to be a rifle. You can't do this with a handgun—can you? No silencer—shit, this guy knew what he was doing. A silencer would have made the shot unpredictable. Only a pro knows shit like that. Where would be the best place to shoot from?* His head swivels, repeating, *thirty degrees, thirty degrees. Shooting from one of those windows in the skyscraper would be problematic. He'd need access and then a way out. The gunfire would attract too much attention, making the escape difficult. Okay, I can rule those out.* His eyes lock on the garage. *It's the garage. Would someone be crazy enough to shoot from there? It's not a controlled area. What if the parking attendant was in on it? Jesus, that would be three people in on it. The list is growing. Still, you can't control everyone already inside the garage. It would be too easy for someone to walk up on you. If not there, where?* He scans the rooflines, returning to the garage. *No, it's the garage.*

Entering the garage, he takes the elevator to level five. He walks, observing the vehicles. *This is too crowded. Was it crowded that day?* He takes the stairs up to level six. His footsteps echo off the walls. Stepping out onto level six, it's the same. He returns to the stairs.

Level seven is different. *This is better—it's like I can breathe, not so busy. Still, I would want something more isolated. Did the shooter care? This dude was a pro. Shit, what if it was a woman? What if he, they, shot from inside a van? That might work. Back it up—maybe he's got a unique window or hatch? Maybe? That would make this operation easier. But would it have given him the sight line he needed?*

He proceeds to level eight, the top level, which is uncovered. Walking to the edge, he peers down. *Good sight line from here. You could make the shot and escape in a vehicle. It's not busy up here—and it's about a thirty-degree angle.* He makes a call.

"Hey Perez, where are you?"

"I'm downtown. We got another gang shooting. Where the hell are you? I thought you were meeting me here. Man, this shit is getting worse. Why?"

"I'm working on the shooting at the hostel."

"Did somethin' break?"

"Nah, not yet. But I need your help. Can you meet me over here?"

"What?" Silence. "Dude . . . Sure, give me forty."

"Great. I'll be waiting at the bar and grill across the street."

Walking up to the bar and grill, Perez stops, peering into the big window of the restaurant; Julian is in a daze, studying the kill site. He shakes his head as he enters the bistro.

Perez interrupts. "Hey man, whatcha looking at?"

Julian jumps. "Oh shit." Their eyes lock.

"You, okay?"

"Yeah, yeah."

"Ya sure? I think I gave you a heart attack."

"No, no, I'm good," Julian replies.

"Okay."

"What's happening downtown?"

"Another gang shooting. At least, that's what it looks like. So, what's up?"

"This case."

"Dude, why are you getting all wrapped up in this one? We got four shootings a week. It's a fuckin' war zone out there."

"Exactly. It's a war zone. But, let me ask you something: how do you know when a shooting is gang-related?"

"Shit, man, that's easy. Bullets everywhere. Usually, a drive-by. You'd think those pinche pendejos would get shooting lessons. Shit, with the money they'd save in ammunition alone, they could all eat at McDonald's for a week—the whole fuckin' gang."

"That's what's bugging me. One shot. One fucking shot."

"Yeah, one shot. So, it's a mob hit."

"Nah, I checked. As far as I can tell, he's not connected. We don't have anything—the Feds don't have anything. Jesus, the dude, coached high school football and then goes fuckin' crazy, shoots up the head coach's wife and family, steals a cab, a security car, and then fuckin' escapes here?"

"Dude, ya need to give up this shit. How about you take, like—a vacation? When was the last time you took any serious time off?"

"I don't know. I can't."

"Jesus. Okay, there's still no connection between him and the truck driver?"

"Nothing, except a crazy tie-breaker event back in Texas—they might have brushed shoulders there. But I got this insight today. What if running him over was a way to give cover for the shooter, you know, so he could get away?"

"Dude—you think the shooter and driver are working together?" Julian nods. "Man, we have fifty murders from people in this town to work on. Isn't the FBI working on this thing?"

"Not yet. I'm guessing we got forty-eight hours. But for some reason, this thing has got me by the balls."

"The word I have is the Feds are stepping in."

"I know."

"Okay, okay. I know you, and you're not going to let this go," Perez remarks. "Why are we here?"

"I'm thinking, how would I assassinate this dude?"

"I give. How?"

"That's what I'm asking."

"Haven't we done this before?"

"Yeah, but let's do it again."

"Jesus, you're a piece of work. Okay, well first, you'd have to know his movements with a degree of certainty."

"Right." Julian flips open his notebook, jotting a few notes.

"It was, what, a thirty-degree entry point?"

"Yeah."

"They would need a perch. Because it was one bullet, I think we can safely say it was one shooter. Right?"

"Exactly," Julian replies.

"And you'd need a clear sight line."

"Right," Julian replies, writing.

"Why are you writing this stuff down?"

"I don't know. It makes me feel better."

"Whatever," Perez replies.

"Because the body was thrown, we don't know exactly where he was standing when he was shot."

"Right. Let's go across the street." Perez says.

"Let's."

The two men cross the street, surveying the area in front of the hostel.

"It's early, and all we know, he was crossing the middle of the street," Julian says.

"Right. He walks out, and he would." Perez points. "He landed over there, right?"

"Right."

"Okay, so he probably got between two cars before he bolted into the street, which means—"

"He didn't get shot until he made it into the street, or he would have been dropped right there."

"Right. If he's crossing right here, where would the shooter be?"

"Right there," Perez points at the garage.

"I was walking that earlier today. Do you think this person would shoot from a parking level?"

"This looks like a pro did it. Right?" Julian nods. "I think he found a nest—how about on top of one of those elevators—wait a second, what is that?" Perez points. "On the other corner?"

"Man, I didn't think of that when I was there. It looks like a stairway."

"Let's go check it out."

They walk the eighth level. Perez snoops by the stairway, while Julian ponders how to get on top of the elevator. They wander back together, meeting at the edge overlooking the street.

"You know, they could have shot from here. It's a quick getaway," Perez remarks.

"Right." Julian gazes down at the hostel.

"Man, it's an easy shot from here."

"That's what I was thinking."

"Did forensics comb this place?"

"I'm not sure. I think so. If they had found anything, we would have heard."

"Yeah." Perez wanders back to the stairway. Opening the door, he looks down the stairs, listens, and then looks up. "Hey man, it's open."

"What?"

Perez climbs the ladder, pushing the hatch open. "Shit." He calls down to Julian. "Hey, get up here."

Julian climbs the ladder. Perez is at the wall, looking down at the hostel.

"Damn," Julian says.

"Damn is right. This is the spot, man. This can't be any more perfect."

"Man, look at that. And it's about thirty degrees. Damn," Julian says.

"You know, one thing that's always bugged me about this—"

"What's that?"

"How did he know he was here?"

"I know. It's been bugging the shit out of me too. He was here, what, a day and a half?"

"Something like that," Perez replies. "He must have been tracking him."

Julian nods. "One shot, one fucking shot. It wasn't a mistake."

"No way, Jose. This was a pro."

"Yep," Julian replies, gazing down at the kill site. "A real pro."

Fred sits in the kitchen, cup in hand, reading the newspaper. Tom stumbles in.

Fred looks over his newspaper. "Good morning."

"Morning," Tom replies. "Oh good, you've made coffee."

"You seem to be getting up later each day."

"I know. I roll over in bed, trying to think of a good reason to get up."

"How about—it's morning?" Fred remarks. Tom chuckles, pouring a cup.

"Hey, do you know this guy who ran over that assistant coach of yours?"

"The one that ran over Pete?"

"Yeah, this William Bates. I guess they call him Billy."

"Nah, I think so."

"Was he at your coin-toss thingy?"

"What a circus—half of the state of Texas was there."

"It says here they're not sure how far Pete's body flew—after impact."

"Pete, a human rocket. I'd like to see that." He chuckles. "I'm glad the son of a bitch is dead," Tom remarks. "I sure won't be shedding any tears. Is that bad of me?"

"Shit, no. He was a piece of shit. Did you know Billy was friends with John Helman?"

"Who?"

"The man that beat the shit out of you."

"Really."

"Yeah, yeah. You think he was settling a score?"

"Maybe—Jesus, that means it's going to come back to me."

"How so?"

"I don't know. Like I hired him?"

"I think your logic is a little off."

"I guess?"

"It's okay. You've gone through a lot, so you're not thinking so clearly."

"Why's that?"

"Why would you have gotten hooked up with a friend of the man who beat the crap out of you? To get him to run over your assistant coach?"

"I guess you're right."

There's a knock at the door. Fred glances at his watch. "Who's that this early?" Fred goes to the front door, looking through the peephole. "Fuck," Fred mumbles. For a moment, he thinks about making a run for it. He opens the door. "Can I help you?"

"Good morning, sir." The agents flash their badges. "We're with the FBI. I'm Agent Walter Hanks, and this is Agent Veronica Broadway." Fred nods. "Is there a Thomas Thompson here?" Relief flushes through Fred's body.

"Sure. You want to come in?"

"That would be great." The agents enter.

Fred yells, "Hey, Tom, company." Fred points at the couch. "Make yourself comfortable. Coffee?"

"That would be great," Walter replies. "Veronica?"

"I'm good, thank you."

"Cream, sugar?" Fred asks.

"A little cream," Walter replies.

"You got it." As they pass, Fred whispers to Tom. "FBI." Tom nods.

"Mr. Thompson?" Walter asks.

"Yes," Tom replies. The agents flash their badges.

"We'd like to ask you some questions—"

"About when I was put in the hospital?"

"Hospital?" Walter replies.

"Yeah, back in Texas. Did you catch the guy?"

"Yes, sir," Veronica replies. "We didn't catch him. He died in a San Antonio hospital."

"He did?"

"He did. We'd like to go through everything with you—if that's okay?" They sit.

"Sure. How did he die?" Tom asks. Fred brings in the coffee; he eavesdrops for a moment before returning to the kitchen.

"It was a combination of things. He was hit in the head, but he was also shot."

"Jesus."

"Mr. Thompson, you died, right?" Veronica asks.

"So, they tell me."

"You don't remember anything?"

"I do. But I won't bore you with the details."

"But you did die?"

"Yep. They said it was a resurrection."

"Resurrection? Wow," Walter remarks. "You don't hear that one much."

"How'd that make you feel? You know, after your resurrection—"

"Are you serious?"

"Yeah, angry, sad, grateful you got another chance at life?"

"You know, no one has asked me that up to now. Most people want to know if there was a light. Or, if I was given a mission."

"Were you—given a mission?" Walter asks.

"Not that I can tell. I seem to be attracting these groupies—I don't know what to call them. Some tell me they're in my flock. Some say I should use them."

"Is one of these people William Bates?"

"That's the guy that ran over Pete Russ—right?" The agents nod. "No, I don't know that person. But as a football coach, I meet a lot of people, so I guess it's possible I've had an encounter with him, but I don't know who that is."

"Do you think he would act as an avenger or a vigilante for your wife's shooting?"

"Hell, I don't know? I meet people who want me to bless their children—or tell them where to invest their money. But this Billy, I don't know him."

"You live an interesting life," Veronica remarks.

"You want to trade lives?"

"You seem a little bitter?"

"Yeah, well, that's my problem."

"Your assistance coach, Pete—"

"Now, there's a piece of work," Tom replies.

"The reports we read indicate he tried to kill you and your wife?" Walter asks.

"He shot at all of us—you can add my kids and father-in-law to that list. My wife took the worst of it—you probably know that."

"Yes, we are sorry to hear that. Why did you hire him? As your assistant coach."

"I didn't. He came along as part of the job. It was like a packaged deal."

"And we understand he harassed you a lot back in Texas?"

"I'll say—"

"How did that make you feel?"

"Mad as hell. It was like he made it his mission to make my life hell. How would that make you feel? And then, he shoots my wife—like I said, a real piece of work."

"Mad enough to kill him?"

"What? I just wanted him to go away," Tom says. "But I'm not sad about what happened to him, if that's what you're asking."

"Do you know anyone who would want to kill Pete? Did he have a lot of enemies?"

"I'm not following. Wasn't he run over?" Tom asks.

Walter clears his throat. "What we're about to tell you has not been released to the press."

"Okay."

"He was also shot," Veronica says.

"Shot? I don't understand. That guy Billy ran him over—Right?"

"True, true, but he was shot at the time he was run over."

"I'm not following."

"It's crazy, but he was shot at the same time I ran him over."

"Jesus. Like bam-bam?"

"Something like that."

"And you want to know if I shot him?"

"No. You were down in Mooresville when all this happened?"

"Yeah, I guess I was. We were all waiting for the word on my wife."

"Right. We were hoping you might identify someone who might have a grudge against him."

"A grudge?"

"Yeah. Someone who might want to kill him."

"Can I ask a question?" Tom asks.

"Sure."

"Do you know why he went to Chicago? I remember sitting in the hospital—after the shooting—it was all over the TV. They were trying to find him, and I thought he was headed to Mexico."

"That is the question, isn't it? Why Chicago?"

"Did you talk to the Sheriff? Down in Big Springs."

"We did."

"If Sam doesn't know, I sure don't. He seemed to have friends back in Texas. But I don't know if anyone had a grudge against him. He was more of an annoyance for me—at least up to the shooting. Did you talk to the barber?"

"Barber?"

"Yeah, Burt. He knows everything about that town. They were very close."

Veronica writes a few notes. "Does he have a last name?"

"Last name? Isn't that crazy? I don't. You know, I never heard anyone ever say his last name. He's just Burt. You should ask Sheriff Duff—he'd know. Burt is easy to find—his name is on the barbershop—Burt's Barbershop. He's there all the time. You know, it's kinda crazy, but maybe he lives there? You got me thinking about things I've never thought about before."

"Okay, we'll investigate it. Thank you for the tip," Walter says.

"You were down in Mooresville for a while?" Veronica asks.

"Yeah, yeah. Finally, they transferred my wife up here."

"Before all this started, did you know John Helman?"

"Not at all. I shake, you know, thinking about him. He was so damn big. He made me feel like a little kid. That's a bad feeling for a grown man."

"I can imagine. Did you say something to provoke him?"

"I'm not sure. I don't remember much except turning around and seeing this huge man. It's all blank after that."

"I'm looking at the list of injuries you sustained that night, and then you had a rapid recovery?" Walter asks.

Brakes screech. There's the sound of doors slamming like machine gun fire. Tom gazes over the agents' shoulders through the big picture window, focusing on the gathering media vehicles. Distracted, Tom still answers the questions while watching the crowd outside grow.

"Yep. They called me the *miracle man*. Damn."

"What?" the agents crane their heads to see what has got Tom's attention.

"They found me."

"What? Who?"

"The media." Tom points. They gander at the media vans gathering. The number swells to fifteen.

"Jesus, look at all of them." Veronica looks at Tom. "You've been dealing with this?"

"Yep, everywhere I go. I did get a little break. Looks like that's over now."

"Huh." She gazes back at the crews setting up. Fred comes out of the kitchen.

"Damn. Here we go," Fred remarks, nestling up to the window, peeking from behind the curtains.

"Mr. Winters, can I ask you a few questions?" Walter asks.

"What?"

"I have a few questions for you."

"Me?" Fred asks. Walter nods. "Okay. Sure."

"You were in the Marine Corps?"

"Yep."

"I understand you were an administrative clerk?"

"Yep, 0151."

"What's that?"

"It was my MOS. You know, my job while I was in."

"I see. Did you ever shoot rifles?"

"It's the Marines—you got to be able to shoot. Ya don't get out of boot camp unless you can shoot."

"And you were in Vietnam?"

"Yep. I was lucky."

"Lucky?"

"Yeah, I served as admin for an artillery battery. Kilo, one eleven, 1st Marines. I was behind a desk. I could have ended up humping a machine gun as some grunt, and then I probably wouldn't be standing in front of you right now. They would have brought my ass back in a body bag."

"Your records state you're qualified as an expert rifleman—what's that mean?"

"It means I can shoot a rifle."

"So that's good, being an expert?"

"Yeah, an expert is the best."

"You were drafted?"

"Nah, I signed up before they could draft me. It was the sixties before the protests started."

"Do you have guns?" Veronica asks.

"Sure, I think I might have a pistol or two around here."

"How about you, Mr. Thompson? Do you own any guns?"

"Nah, never have."

"Okay, so can we see your pistols, Mr. Winters?"

"Sure, but why?"

"I'm looking to cross people off the list."

"What list?" Fred asks.

"Anyone that might have a reason to kill Pete Russ."

"Wasn't he run over?"

"He was, but as we were telling your son-in-law, and this is hush-hush, he was also shot."

"Shot? How the hell does that work?"

"We're keeping it quiet while we investigate. Your pistols?"

"Ahh. I keep them out back in the shed."

"None here, in the house?"

"Nah, not in the house. The grand kids are here a lot."

"Oh," Veronica replies.

"So, your pistols?" Walter asks.

"Sure, let's go out back," Fred says, pointing.

Fred unlocks the heavy-duty padlock, opening the door to the shed. Fred leads the agents inside.

"Wow, this is a nice shed," Walter says.

"It's more like a little house," Veronica remarks.

"Yeah, but it doesn't have a bathroom or kitchen," Fred replies.

"What is this place?" Walter asks.

"It's kinda my special place. I guess they call them man-caves these days. I built it back when the wife was around, and my daughter was young."

"You only have one daughter?" Veronica asks.

"Yep."

"How are you doing with her shooting?"

"Mad as hell. Breaks my heart."

"And the man that did the shooting?"

"I'm glad the son of a bitch is dead," Fred replies. The agents look at each other.

"Those are strong words," Walter says.

"Yeah. How would you feel if someone shot up someone you love?"

"True, true," Walter replies. "Keeping your pistols back here, that doesn't help if you need them for protection."

"True, but the grand kids are over a lot, like I said. I'd hate for something wacky to happen, and one of them got hurt. I'm sure I don't have to tell you the statistics of people getting injured by their own weapons," Fred remarks.

"No, no, you don't. Why do you have them?"

"I like to shoot them. It's a form of meditation for me. I guess it's something I picked up from the Corps." Fred opens the gun safe. He pulls out each pistol, placing them on the table for the agents to inspect. Walter picks up one.

"I thought you said you only had two?" Veronica asks.

"Ahh, two, four, what's the difference?"

"I see you have two forty-fives and two nine millimeters?"

"Yeah, yeah," Fred replies.

"Which one is your favorite?"

"That nine-millimeter in your hand."

Walter holds it up like he's going to take a shot. "Yeah, it's got a nice balance to it."

"Do you go to the range a lot?" Veronica asks.

"I don't know if it's a lot? But yes, from time to time."

"Do you ever shoot rifles?"

"Sure, from time to time," Fred replies.

"But you don't have one right now?" Walter asks.

"Nah, I sold my last one a while back. Although I was considering getting a new rifle, but, no, only the pistols."

"Where do you go?" Veronica asks. Fred is ready for this question.

"I go to B&D and sometimes Para Armory," Fred replies. He doesn't tell them about Tremont Rod Gun Club, which is the only place he practiced with his rifles.

"Nice weapons, Mr. Winters," Walter says, placing the pistol on the table. "You got anything, Broadway?"

"Nah, I'm good."

Two

Billy

Billy sneaks into his house; he doesn't want to talk to his mother. His mother watches TV. She hears him—caught.

Peggy bellows out, "Out making a name for yourself?"

He jumps, tensing before relaxing. "You heard?"

"Hell, it's all over the damn TV. You're a Goddamn movie star." Billy scowls. "Those Rangers were here looking for your ass."

"Rangers? What? When?"

"Hell, I don't know. It's when ya disappeared. I told them to tell ya: we're out of milk. Ya got milk?"

"Nah."

"I'm guessin' ya haven't seen them."

"Nah."

"Chicago?" She asks.

"Uh-huh."

"Ya ran over someone?"

"Uh-huh."

"What ya into, boy?"

"Nothin.'"

"If ya say so—we need milk."

"Okay. Anything else?"

Billy doesn't make a run for milk. He goes to The Cue Ball; business is light. He snuggles up to the bar, sitting on his regular bar stool.

"Hey, Billy."

"Hey, Tim."

"Where ya been?"

"You don't know?"

"Of course, I do, but I thought I'd let you tell the story. Chicago, is what I'm hearing?"

"Yeah—it was cold as shit. I've never seen so much snow."

"Snow? Was the dude you ran over really from Texas?"

"I guess. They put me in this interrogation room."

"What are you talking about—an interrogation room?" Billy nods. "Why?"

"The dude got shot."

"What ya talkin' about?"

"The dude was shot—I don't know why it's not on the news, but the dude was shot. I thought they were going to lock my ass up."

"Whatcha talkin' about? Didn't you run him over?"

"No, no. I ran him over, but he was also shot—like, simultaneously."

"You're shittin' me?"

"Serious as a heart attack. Shit, I didn't see anything—and I mowed him down. It was some crazy shit. They took my truck, my gun, and put me in the back of a cop car. Shit, I was in the back of that car for like two hours, and then they put me in this room. I don't even know how long I was there, but it was long. They were just fuckin' with me."

"Jesus, Billy, sounds like a hell of an experience. Why would someone want to shoot him? Didn't he coach football?"

"I guess. I didn't find out until they released me, but he shot up that head coach's family. Maybe one of them shot him?"

"Wait a second. I'm a little fuzzy on this, but he was from Texas, and he shot up the family, like—"

"In Indiana."

"Right. And you ran him over in Chicago—"

"Right."

"How in the fuck would anyone know he was in Chicago?"

"I know, right? Fuckin' weird."

"Man, this is some crazy shit. What's it like, fate or some shit?"

"Ya got me? I was floored when I found out the dude was from Texas."

"Shit." Tim stares at Billy. "Maybe the dude did more than coach football?"

"Maybe."

"Jesus, Billy." They share a look. "Ya sure have gotten sucked into some crazy shit lately."

"You can say that again. I'm tellin' ya, when I was in that room, I thought I was never going to see Texas again."

"Well, someone must be watching out for ya, cause you're here." They laugh. "Beer?"

"Yeah, set me up."

Tim pours a glass, placing it on a coaster.

"Hey dude, all kinds of people are looking for ya," Tim says.

"I heard. The Rangers?"

"Yeah, them, and Sylvia, oh, and Brett."

"Damn. Maybe I shouldn't have come back?"

"I thought ya liked Sylvia?"

"I do, but it's been wonky since John died. It's probably my fault."

A voice booms from behind Billy. "What the fuck, dude?"

Billy swivels on his bar stool. "Brett."

"Don't *Brett* me." Brett points. "Out back—I need to talk to your ass."

Brett leads Billy toward the back door. As soon as Billy clears the doorway, Brett drives his forearm into Billy's chest. Billy's back collides with a brick wall, sounding like slapping meat hitting a wall. Billy is pinned. He coughs.

In a wispy voice, Billy says, "Damn dude, what the hell?"

"Dude, what did you do?" Brett asks. Billy tries to free himself; he looks like a bug stuck on its back. Billy's face turns different shades of red as he struggles to breathe.

He struggles to speak, eking out, "Chill, man."

"Man, Skinny is all up in my ass, asking about you and what I told ya." Brett releases Billy. He paces like a caged big cat. Billy throws his hands on his knees, coughing.

His voice returns. "How in the fuck does he know about me?"

"It's complicated."

"Okay, okay. So, he knows. Dude, it's okay—really."

Brett stops, giving him a deadeye stare. "It's not fuckin' okay, man. Skinny is fuckin' psycho. You never know what that motherfucker is going to do. He's fuckin' scary—shit" He goes back to pacing. "This is bad, man. If he finds out, you—" He stops, locking eyes with Billy. "You need to leave town."

"Whatcha talkin' about? I'm good. I can take care of myself."

"Dude, you're not getting it—and now the fuckin' Rangers have also been sniffin' around, and they're all up in my ass. Dude, I don't need this shit. Fuck."

"Rangers? Oh shit, that is bad. Those boys just like fuckin' with me. Look, man, I will go to my grave with what you told me," Billy says.

"Fuck, fuck. Billy—"

"Look, man; I get it. I get it."

"Can ya like—take another vacation?"

"Dude, it's okay. Really."

"All these motherfuckers are squeezing me."

"Ya want me to talk to Skinny?"

"Bad idea, man. Bad idea. You need to, like—disappear."

The Rangers enter Burt's Barbershop. Burt cuts Paul Johnson's hair—what's left of it.

"Howdy, boys," Burt says. "I'm almost done here, and I'll be with ya in a sec."

"Take your time," Don replies, plopping his ass down in a chair in front of the big picture window. He picks up a magazine while Jim examines the bulletin board. Jim sees Ann Collins' signature.

"Ann Collins was here?" Jim asks.

"Huh? Oh, yeah, now there's a beauty," Burt remarks.

"Who's Ann Collins?" Don asks.

"She's the nurse—"

"It's the coach's upgrade," Burt remarks.

"Upgrade?" Paul asks.

"Yeah, the one the coach has been running around with," Burt replies.

"She was here?" Paul asks.

"Yep," Burt replies.

Jim turns, glancing at the TV; they're reporting on Billy running over Pete.

"When was this?" Paul asks.

"He coached here, didn't he?" Jim asks.

"What?" Burt replies.

Jim points to the TV. "That guy—the one that got run over, what's his name?"

"Pete Russ," Burt replies.

"Yeah, that's the one, Pete Russ. He coached here, didn't he?" Jim asks. Don peeks over the top of his magazine, eyeing Burt and Paul.

"He sure did," Burt replies.

"Word has it, y'all were like *special* friends?" Jim asks. Burt stops, dropping his comb and scissors to his side.

"I guess ya could say that?" Burt replies. Paul is happy to listen.

"How would you say it?" Jim asks.

"Let's see—"

"The way I hear it, y'all would like to cook up things, and I'm not talking barbecue," Jim says.

"I don't know—"

"Weren't you in on the house thing that happened a while back? At the Thompson's house?"

"Well ... Um ... Whatcha fellas want?" Burt asks.

Don chimes in. "I think what my partner is driving at is y'all were a bit social, beyond cutting his hair."

"Am I in trouble here?" Burt asks.

"I don't know. Are ya?" Jim replies.

"Did ya cook up that event at the Thompson house with him?" Don asks.

"I think I'm going to have to ask you fellas to leave," Burt says.

"Okay, if that's the way you want to play it. We can call you in, official-like, if that's what you want?" Jim asks. Burt pauses.

Paul whispers, "I think I'd talk to them, Burt."

Burt nods. "What exactly do ya fellas want to know?"

"We understand Pete Russ was your special project," Jim says.

"I think Mr. Johnson can confirm that," Don says, staring at Paul. Paul turns red. "Ya see that? Embarrassment—I'm going to take that as a big yes."

"Now, I had nothing to do with what happened at the Thompson house," Burt says.

"Relax, we don't care about that. That's a local issue. We want to know if you knew Pete was going to Indiana to shoot up the Thompsons?" Jim asks. "Was that the plan?"

"Well ... I ... Ahh—"

"Word has it y'all were scheming to get Coach Thompson back to coach here next year, but the funny thing is, weren't ya trying to get Mr. Russ placed as the head coach?" Jim asks. Burt feels the glare burning from the Ranger's eyes as if they were peeking into his soul.

"Well ... Ahh—"

"Mr. Johnson, do ya want to chime in here?" Don asks.

"I think Burt can tell you what he was doin'."

"Okay. Burt," Don says.

"I was tryin' to keep the boy out of jail. When charges went to criminal, I thought, and he agreed, if we got Coach Thompson back, he, or his wife, might drop the charges against him."

"That's what you two were up to?" Paul asks.

"Well . . . Yeah."

"Damn, Burt, why are ya always tryin' ta fix things?" Paul asks.

"Burt, what about Indiana? Did you know?" Don asks.

"Now hold on here a cotton-picking minute, I told him to send Skinny—"

"Skinny?" Jim asks.

"Yeah, but he went himself. The boy lost his fool-headed mind. He must've snapped."

"I see . . . Do you know Billy Bates?" Jim asks.

"Who?" Burt asks.

"Billy Bates, the man that ran Pete over in Chicago?"

"Nah, I don't know him. Is he from around here?" Burt asks.

"Nah, down south a bit."

"One thing is for sure," Paul says. "If Burt says he doesn't know someone, he doesn't know him."

"Did you know all this was goin' on, Mr. Johnson?"

"I hadn't a clue. But now that you mention it, I did think something was up when Burt changed his tune about the coach."

The Rangers sit in their SUV, marinating on their powwow with Burt.

"Whatcha think?" Jim asks.

Don strokes his chin. "I think this all stinks to the high heavens."

"Yeah, I'm with you. I think we need to find out who this Skinny is."

Don nods. "Yep. That's for sure."

Jim points. "The Sheriff's office is right there."

"Okay, let's go talk to the good Sheriff. What's his name?"

"Sam Duff." The Rangers exit the SUV and take fifty steps to the Sheriff's office.

"Howdy, gentleman," JR says.

"Howdy." They tip their hats.

"How can I help ya?" JR asks.

"Is the Sheriff in?" Jim asks.

"He stepped out for a bit. Something about the hardware store. He'll be back shortly, or at least that's what he told me. I can tell 'em y'all are here?"

"That would be great."

"He's gonna want to know why."

"We're here about Billy Bates," Jim says.

"Billy? The one that ran over Pete Russ?" JR asks.

"You know him?"

"Nah, only what I've picked up from the news."

"Do ya know Skinny?" Don asks.

"Sure, everyone around these parts knows Skinny."

"Does he have a last name?"

"Sure. It's Hart. His real name is Theodore Fredrick Hart."

"I can see why he might want to go by Skinny. Do you know where we might locate Mr. Hart?"

"He lives in a mobile home down by the crick, on the south side of town. Let me rustle up his address for y'all. Just so ya know, it's a rough drive in."

"Good to know," Don remarks. "Did Skinny and Pete Russ know each other?"

JR hands a post-it note to Don. "Hell yeah. *Thick as thieves,* those two."

"Do tell."

"Hell, those two were always cookin' up somethin'. I think Skinny would do anything for Pete. Skinny always did the dirty work, if y'all get what I'm driving at?" The Rangers nod. "I'll get the Sheriff."

"Thank you kindly," Don says.

"Do y'all know how the coach's wife is doin'?" JR asks.

"From what I understand, they moved her up to Cleveland."

"It's a shame about her. I still can't believe Pete went postal like that."

"Ya know what they say? Ya never really know someone."

"Yeah, I guess?"

Sam enters. Don and Jim stand.

"Howdy, boys," Sam says. They tip their hats.

"Howdy."

"I hope JR has been treatin' ya well, while y'all have been waitin'?" Sam asks.

"He has," Don replies. "Good man, ya got there."

"We like him. Let's mosey back to my office," Sam says. Sam shuts the door. "Have a seat, and state what's on your fellas mind."

"We're working up a background on Pete Russ—for the FBI. Any insight ya might have would be much appreciated."

"I see. Pete is an interesting sort. Kind of a whiner. He's one of those that thinks everyone is out to get him, if ya know what I mean." The Rangers nod. "But he also pushes if he doesn't get what he wants. The combination seems to always get his ass in hot water."

"What was the deal with Coach Thompson?"

"That poor man, he never had a clue about the shitstorm he was steppin' into."

"How so?" Jim asks.

"Pete wanted to be the head coach somethin' awful, and thought Tom Thompson was the reason he wasn't the head coach. What Pete failed to realize is that even if Thompson left, he wasn't going to be a head coach; he's not a leader. For him, it was always about him. Paul Johnson knew this, so he found Tom and brought him in as the coach.

Boy, oh boy, what a mess. I advised Paul not to do it. Bringing in an outsider was goin' to be nothin' but trouble."

"And, all this stuff we're hearing about the Thompson house—"

"That was Pete trying to push him out. Pete got a bunch of kids to trash his house. The kids thought it was fun, but things got out of hand. I'm guessin' you heard about the brick?" The Rangers nod. "Anyway, someone could have been killed—the sitter and coaches' kids were in that room. It probably would have been a non-event, except for the brick. The brick changed everything—got Pete's ass in a sling."

"How does this Skinny fit into the picture?"

"Skinny? Ya gotta watch out for Skinny. Only people in these parts know that Skinny was the quarterback for one of the State Championship teams here. He thought he was goin' to the NFL. Texas U recruited him. He blew out his knee and ended up back here. Something happened to the boy through all that. Anyway, Pete Russ was on that championship team with him, and they've been friends for as long as I can remember. They had a bond thicker than blood if ya ask me. If ya have any contact with Skinny, be on guard. He's very unpredictable. I think the boy has been dippin' into the special barbecue sauce, but I can't prove it. He always has money, but he barely works. He's slicker than a hog in mud. Like I said, I can't catch him."

"We've been told Skinny would do the dirty work for Pete?" Jim asks.

"Yep, I'd say that's right. When this Thompson house thing broke, I had all kinds of people turn on Pete, but no one turned on Skinny—I know he was the ringmaster, but Skinny scares the hell out of people, so everyone kept their trap shut about him."

Three

Take a Left Up Here

Tom watches, the curtain gives him cover as he peeks at the crowd in front of the house. Fred approaches from behind.

"Tom, we can't live like this." Tom glances at him before returning his gaze to the media circus.

"I know."

"Whatcha gonna do about it?"

"I got a plan."

"Are those your groupies traipsing all over the yard?"

"I guess? I only know a few of them. That looks like Lester right there," Tom draws his phone to his ear.

"Hello."

"Laura, this is Tom Thompson."

"Tom. How are you?"

"I wish I could say I'm good, but—"

"You certainly have a lot swirling around you."

"You see that?"

"I do."

"I still don't know how this works. Anyway, I keep saying to myself: *this is my life now*. But if this truly is my life now, it suc—ah, never mind. Hey, I need some input."

"I've been keeping tabs on you—hope that's okay?"

"Someone's got to do it. Sorry, no, that's great."

"Good. From what I'm getting, this chaos will continue for a while. Unless you do something bold."

"Great. Bold. Like what?"

"It's time for you to steer the boat."

"Someone else told me that. Not in those exact words, but you know—"

"So, you've sought counsel?"

"Yes."

"This is good. A left turn, so to speak, is coming," Laura says.

"Haven't I had enough of those? I'm mean, if you get enough left turns, aren't you going in circles?"

She chuckles. "Good to keep your humor. But, unlike the other ones, this one won't be so dramatic."

"Is that good?"

"I'm sure you've heard this before, or maybe something like it, but it's served me well. It's not what comes at you that's important—it's how you react to it."

"Yeah, yeah. That's a good one. I also like the *Rocky* one."

"Rocky?"

"The movie?"

"Oh. I've never seen it."

"Yeah, it goes something like, life's not about how hard you can hit, but how hard you can get hit and still keep moving forward."

"Huh . . . Rocky, I like that. That certainly has been your life in a nutshell lately."

"Yep. Reflecting on it helps. Anyway, you mentioned something about virtual reality?"

"Yes, I did. I've been told this is the best way to launch yourself, so to speak."

"What am I launching?"

"All these people you've been collecting, they need focus—a purpose—inspiration."

"You mean my groupies?"

"Some call them your flock."

"Okay, whatever."

"You need a platform to speak to them, guide them. They can be very helpful to you in your next chapter."

"Okay, but I don't know anything about technology."

"I see that, but there is someone close to you that does. Tap them."

"Like on the shoulder?"

"If you want to think of it that way. They will be more than willing to help."

"How do I find them?"

"As far as I see, they're around you right now."

"They are? I don't know what to do with these people. It's like herding cats."

"Tom, you're the perfect person for this."

"For what? What is *this*?"

"You were brought back to help restore the truth. You haven't figured that out?"

"I was never told this when I, well, you know."

"Sure, you were."

"I was?"

"Yeah. Help would be presented in your time of need."

"Christ . . . Okay, so I have to find this technology guy or person."

"That's what's up next. You need to have this all in place before you go on television. You sound angry."

"No, I'm sorry. It's more frustration. It's the media people, and the groupies—the flock, whatever. I just want some peace."

"One step at a time."

"One step—I can do that. Okay. Thank you."

Tom returns to watch the circus out front. Before all this chaos, he would never have called a psychic for advice. My how things have changed. He makes another call.

"Hello."

"Lester."

"Mr. Thompson?"

"Call me Tom."

"Okay, Tom. How are you?"

"Well—"

"I get it. It's crazy out here. Are you in the house?"

"I'm looking right at you." Lester turns, looking. "Can you come to the back patio?"

"Sure. I'll be there in a sec."

Lester stands waiting. Tom slides open the door.

"Man, it's cold out there," Lester says, shaking off the cold.

"How long have you been out there?"

"Long enough."

"Have a seat. Would you like some coffee or something hot to drink?"

"Oh man, coffee would be great." Tom sets him up.

"I think this conversation is way overdue."

"I agree, but you've had a lot on your plate."

"Thank you for waiting. What is this GoFundMe thing?"

"I set up a GoFundMe account for you online. It crossed a million dollars this morning."

"What? Did you say a million, like with an M?"

"Yep."

"What's this for?"

"Anything you need, really, but mainly for any medical bills."

"Really . . . Amazing . . . Are you good with technology?" Tom asks.

"Maybe. It depends on what we're talkin' about."

"Virtual reality."

"VR . . . Huh—"

"What?"

"It's . . . I can help with like websites, stuff like that, but VR is outside my wheelhouse."

"Okay. Do you know anyone?"

"Maybe. I'll have to get back to you on that one."

Tom stands at Ester's sliding glass door. She pulls back the curtain. Their eyes lock. They smile as she slides open the door.

"Oh, Tommy. Come in, come in. You brought the circus with you."

"I know. Sorry about that."

"It's okay. It's only a problem when I need to go somewhere, which isn't often. They got the whole damn street plugged up. Anyway, enough of me bitching. How have you been?"

"I don't know. This crap is getting so old. I'm reaching my limit. Of course, I've thought that before."

"You do seem a bit edgy."

"I know. Sorry. I need your counsel."

"Whatcha got?"

"Oprah is coming up, and that psychic Laura tells me I need to set up some kind of VR, but I don't know the first thing about it, and I don't know anyone who does."

"Sure, you do."

"I do?"

"Yeah. Me."

"You?"

"Uh-huh. I've been learning. It's fun. I'm kind of a techno-geek. My son has been teaching me. I'm not that great at it, but he is. He has all the equipment."

"He does?"

"Why don't we take a road trip to his place? I'll set it up. We're going to have to figure out a way to sneak you out of the house."

"Oh, I can take care of that."

Fred's blood pressure rises as he spies on the circus. *Damn, there's more of them than before. This shit has got to end.*

Tom walks up, surprising Fred. "Checking out the show?"

"You're back," Fred remarks.

"Yeah."

"You said you have a plan for this?"

"I do."

"When does it go into effect—next Christmas?"

"No. By the end of the week, I'll be going on Oprah."

"Oprah. That's still four days away."

"Yeah."

"Can you, like, go to Texas until then?"

"I guess, but the kids, Kathy—"

"Hell, we'll be fine. Make it flashy."

"What?"

"You're leaving. You know, so they know you're gone. Like when you and your girlfriend escaped from her house—that was pretty damn flashy."

Tom ponders. *That was flashy.* "Okay, I think I can arrange that." Tom makes a call. "Hi, it's me."

"I've been wondering about you. Are you okay?" Ann asks.

"Not really. I'm a bit edgy—these people are irritating the crap out of me."

"What people?"

"The media—the groupies. Anyway, I need to be extracted. Do you have my father-in-law's address?"

"I sure do. When can you be ready?"

A big white limo pulls up in front of Ester's house, attracting the attention of all in an eyeshot. Lester rounds up a crew of twenty people, and they migrate toward Ester's front yard. Tom emerges with a small bag. Ester emerges, locking the door. The reporters rush toward Tom. Lester's crew maintains a buffer as Tom and Ester make their way to the limo. There's shouting, the reporters trying to get Tom's attention. Cameras click. The video cameras are taping. This is a scene that would be at home in Los Angeles. The chauffeur has the back door open, and

Tom, Ester, and Lester climb in. Ann waits, smiling, greeting all as they enter. She's armored up with her sunglasses and gloves. Ann and Tom share a moment; they don't dare kiss. Removing her glove, she offers her hand to Ester.

"Hi, I'm Ann."

"You sure are. So nice to finally meet you. I've heard so much about you," Ester replies, glancing at Tom. "Why are you two equipped with sunglasses on such a cloudy day?"

"Safety," Tom replies. Ann nods. "Ann, this is Lester."

"Lester. Nice to meet you." They settle in.

"It's an honor, ma'am." They shake.

"Okay, enough with that ma'am crap," Ann remarks.

Lester smiles. "I'm not sure why you asked me along."

"You've been so helpful," Tom says. "I thought you might want to, like . . . I don't know, be a manager of sorts."

"Manager? What does that mean?"

"I'm not sure at this point. I'm making things up as we go. I certainly need someone to manage this GoFundMe account you started, and you seem to know a lot of the players in your world. I don't know, help me vet people and situations. I was told I needed counsel, so you all are my counsel."

"I see. Well, okay then," Lester replies. "Where are we going?"

"To see Ester's son about this VR thing."

"You found someone—great."

The limo is on the move, nudging the crowd. A path opens, and the limo makes a break for it. The media circus packs up to give chase. It's as if a vacuum cleaned the street.

Fred watches. *You sure are full of surprises, Tom.*

Four
Did You Get the Memo?

Julian reviews the security footage from the garage. The eighth-floor camera hadn't worked for months. The pay booth camera is all he has. He reviews the footage around the time of the shooting. Three cars exited. He checks the license plates against the DMV records. One car, he couldn't match. The driver wore a baseball cap and sunglasses. Perez enters.

"Hey," Perez says. Julian gives him a quick glance.

"Hey."

"Whatcha got?"

"Take a look."

Perez reviews each car. "That's it? This is the only camera?"

"Yep. What do you see?"

"Shit, I don't know, man," Perez replies.

"There are no vans."

"What does that mean? Are we looking for a van? What, did you get a tip?"

"Nah, I was wondering if they might have driven a van."

"Oh. What about this one? He's the guy. Don't ya think?"

Julian leans back in his chair, stroking his chin. "But you can't tell shit from this footage. I can't match the plate."

"He probably replaced the plate."

"I don't know," Julian remarks. "I'm getting loopy."

"Wait a second. What's that?"

"What? Do you see something?"

"Back that up. Okay, hold it—there."

"What?"

"Is that tape?"

"What?"

"Yeah, I think it's colored tape. Look, he covered some digits, and altered others."

"Oh shit. Damn, you're right. Whoever this is, we're dealing with one cagey-ass person."

"Looks like we're dealing with a guy." Perez shifts in his chair. "Haven't the Feds taken this case over?"

"Yep. Yesterday," Julian remarks.

"What the hell, man? Let them mess with this shit."

"I think we're dealing with a paid hit man."

"It sure looks like it. Dude, are you trying to start a war with the Feds?"

The gravel crunches underneath Ranger's boots as they walk. In the distance, a chainsaw buzzes like an annoying insect. There's a light breeze. They stop, inspecting Skinny's mobile home.

"Nice spot," Jim remarks. Don utters a grunt. Due to the chainsaw, they don't hear the crunching tires from the approaching car. A dust cloud drifts over them, catching Jim's attention. He turns. A piss-yellow Cadillac sits with a blonde woman staring at them. The chainsaw stops.

Jim nudges Don. "Hey, Don." Don turns, shouldering up with Jim. It's like a showdown in the old west.

"Fuck me," Tracy mutters. "Rangers. Jesus, Skinny, what did you do this time?" She kills the engine and steps out of the car. "Howdy." She shuts the door. "Y'all looking for Skinny?"

"Howdy, ma'am," Don replies. "Ah, yes. We'd like to have a chat if that's possible?"

She clenches her jaw before answering. "He lit out of here the other night. He does that." She goes about her business, walking to the back of the car. Opening the trunk, she hoists two grocery bags by the handles, setting them on the ground.

"I see," Don replies. They move toward her.

"Would ya like some help with that?" Jim asks.

"Nah. I'm good," she says, closing the trunk lid. She picks up the bags and walks toward them.

"No word on where he might be?" Don asks.

"Nah, he comes and goes—there's a lot of going lately," Tracy brushes by them. She stops and turns. "Ya can come in and wait if ya want, but it could be a long wait." Jim eyes Don. Don pulls a card from his wallet. "Throw it in the bag. I suppose y'all want me to tell 'em y'all were by?"

"Ahh, yes ma'am, if ya could?"

She nods. The Rangers tip their hats as they climb into their SUV. She watches them drive off. Safely out of view, she enters the home. Inside, she places the bags on the counter.

She yells, "Okay, they're gone."

Skinny emerges from the closet. "Did they say what they wanted?" He's nervous like a Jack Russell terrier. He stabs the blinds, peeking.

"Nah, I got their card in the bag."

"Shit." He glances at the bag before peeking out the window again. A cloud of dust hangs in the air.

"What's up, Skinny?"

"I'm not sure?"

"Is this about your ride to Chicago?"

"Maybe?"

"What if it's about the drugs?"

"Nah. They would have had a search warrant if it was that."

"I think ya need to cool it for a while."

"I think you're right."

The limo stops; a private jet awaits. Tom and Ann emerge from the limo. Lester and Ester remain in the car. They wave. Tom and Ann watch the car drive off.

"Easy, fella. Wait until we're on the plane," Ann says.

Tom glances at the Learjet. "Right. That VR stuff is pretty interesting."

"I'll say. I'll have to send a thank you card to your father-in-law."

"For the VR?"

"For getting your ass out of the house and back into my arms." They laugh. "Have you called to find out if this all worked?"

"I will—when we're on the plane."

"So . . . I was thinking," Ann says.

"Uh-huh. Off riding again? Like old times."

"You read my mind."

"Where to this time?"

"How about the Virgin Islands?"

"You brought that place up before. You must really like it?"

"You'll see."

"Is it worth going there for only three days?"

"Oh, yeah," Ann remarks.

"God, I've missed you . . . Okay, let's do it." Tom makes a call as they scale the stairs. "Hey. This is Tom."

"Hey."

"How are things? Did it work?"

"Boy, did it," Fred replies. "Even your flock is gone."

"Excellent. I'm hoping things will calm down after Oprah."

"Yeah, right. I guess you can always dream. If you want to come back to the house, give me a heads up—so I can prepare, you know, psychologically." Fred chuckles.

"Right. Okay, later." Tom takes a seat.

"Everything okay?"

"Yep. Does this plane have a bed?"

"Of course." They smile. "Keep your sunglasses on until we're in the air."

Five

Slippin' Out the Back, Jack

Skinny slips through the backdoor like a ninja, hugging the wall. He's even surprised how quiet he is. Working his way within inches of Brett, who sits at the kitchen table. Skinny pauses, watching Brett; he can reach out and pull Brett's hair. Brett, unaware, reads a sailing magazine and sips from his coffee cup. Brett stops; it's like he's receiving an incoming message. He cocks his head. *Is that breathing?* Brett scoots the chair back to rise. Skinny pounces, striking the back of Brett's neck Brett's face smacks into the table, forcing the coffee cup and magazine to fly; the cup shatters—coffee splatters in all directions.

Like being jolted out of a dream, Brett is clueless about who is attacking him. Skinny tackles Brett—they tumble to the floor. Brett twists to his feet, facing his assailant. *Skinny?* Skinny lunges, clamping down on Brett's neck. Brett clamps down on Skinny's arm—Skinny shoves, ramming Brett into the wall. *Fuck, how can this skinny-ass bitch be so strong?* Skinny is like a Tasmania Devil with an unrelenting attack. Skinny kicks Brett's leg; they tumble to the floor. They struggle. Skinny is on top, plunges his knee into Brett's stomach. Brett grunts. Snatching his ice pick from his back pocket, Skinny pressing it flat on Brett's cheek, just below his eye. Brett freezes, trembling.

"What the fuck, dude?" Skinny barks. "Why the hell are the Rangers sniffing around my house?" Brett tries to swallow—he's got no spit. Skinny grip is crushing Brett's neck; Brett struggles breathe. Brett doesn't hear a word Skinny says; the ice pick has his attention. "You better start talking ya piece of shit, or I'll fuckin' blind you,"

Brett utters a squeak—no words. Skinny knees him in the balls.

"Oh fuck," Brett groans. "Damn, man."

"I thought that might get ya talkin.'"

"What? Shit, man. Chill."

Skinny tightens his grip around Brett's neck. Brett's face turns a beautiful shade of red as a vein in his forehead bulges. "Don't tell me to fuckin' chill." Skinny eases up on the neck.

"Fuck! What do you want?"

"Why are the Rangers snooping around my house?"

"Fuck if I know."

"It's Billy, isn't it? First, he runs over Pete, and now he's gunning to take me out? He's gunning for me, isn't he?"

"What?"

"This Billy ya told me about. He wants to fuck my shit up, doesn't he?"

"What are you talking about?"

"Where can I find him?"

Brett coughs. "Fuck, I don't know?" Skinny clamps down on his neck. His face turns red.

"Where the fuck can I find him? And don't tell me you don't know." He eases up on his neck.

"Shit, man. Try The Cue Ball."

"The Cue Ball? What the fuck is a Cue Ball?"

"It's a bar."

"A bar. Fuck." Skinny tightens his grip. "Quit fuckin' with me! Where does he live?"

"I don't know, man. I see him at The Cue Ball."

"Shit. Does he live there?"

"No. But he goes there—a lot."

"Fuck. Who knows where this motherfucker lives?"

"Sylvia. She knows."

"Sylvia. Where do I find this bitch?"

"She works there."

"At The Cue Ball?"

"Yeah."

"Sounds like a damn popular place. What, do they sell cots?" Skinny releases Brett. Brett scoots to a sitting position, massaging his neck. "The Cue Ball." Skinny jabs the ice pick into Brett's thigh. The pain jolts through his body like twenty-thousand volts.

"FUCK," Brett screams, clutching his leg. He rocks on the floor.

"That's a taste—ya better not be lying to me, or I'll come back and really fuck your shit up." Skinny stands. "I'd go to the hospital for that. I mean, ya don't want to bleed out here on the kitchen floor." Skinny grabs a towel, wiping the ice pick clean. He chuckles, tossing the towel on Brett. "Thanks. It's important to keep your tools clean." Skinny leaves the way he came.

Skinny trolls the streets, hunting for The Cue Ball; it's more complicated than he thought. *How hard can it be to find a bar in this little shithole of a town? Main Street, they got to have a Main Street.* A man standing on the street corner, waiting to cross. He pulls up, lowering his window.

"Howdy."

"Howdy."

"I was wondering if ya could help me?"

"What ya need?" the man asks.

"I'm looking for a place called The Cue Ball?"

The man eases closer, dipping his head. "That's a sweet ride ya got there."

"Yeah, I like it."

"What year is that?"

"Sixty-nine. Completely restored."

"Damn. How much did that cost?"

"A lot. I'd rather not say," Skinny replies.

The man steps back, admiring the car. "Ya don't see cars like this one much."

"No, I can't say that you do. Everybody in these parts seems to drive trucks. About The Cue Ball?"

"Oh shoot, sorry. Ahh, yeah, yer real close." He points. "Up at that corner, take a right. Ya can't miss it."

"Okay. Thank you kindly."

Driving to the corner, he takes a right. *And there it is.* He parks, studying the outside. *Now, how am I going to find this guy? I'm not even sure what he looks like.* He's seen Billy's picture on the news, but that was a while back. *I hope you're home, Sylvia.*

Entering, music plays in the background. Before his eyes adjust to the low light, a voice calls out, "Skinny?"

Was that my name? Skinny searches. *Who's calling my name?*

"What the hell, man?" The voice gets closer. "Skinny, what ya doin' here?"

Skinny's eyes adjust, a large man moves toward him; he looks familiar. *Do I know this guy?* He's having trouble placing him.

Skinny? Swiveling on his stool, Billy watches the reunion. *Is that Brett's Skinny?* Billy didn't know what Skinny looked like, and Skinny is a common name, so it might not be Brett's Skinny.

"Aaron?" Skinny asks, head half-cocked.

"Hell yeah, man! What the hell ya doin' at The Cue Ball?"

"Ya live here?"

"Yeah, man, down the road a bit," Aaron replies, pointing. "Good ta see your ass. Come over and meet some people. Ya want a beer or something? What ya drinking?"

"Ahhh, how about tequila?"

"Shit. Okay. Why the hell not?" Aaron circles his finger in the air. "Hey, Tim, a round of Jose for my table." Aaron wraps his arm around Skinny. "Damn man, great ta see your ass."

"I sure wasn't expecting to see ya here."

"Why are ya here? No one ever comes to Sterling City."

"I'm looking for this dude. Brett told me he hangs here."

Brett? Oh, fuck, it's him. Billy's eyes dart to the front door and then the back, looking for an escape. He decides on the back door that way he can make it look like he's headed to the john.

"Where is Brett? I haven't seen his ass in here in a while."

"I don't know that one?"

"Who ya looking for? Maybe I can help?"

"Billy."

"Billy? Billy Bates?"

"Yeah, that's him."

"Hell man, he's sitting—" Aaron points to the bar. A half-empty glass of beer sits—alone. "Well shit, he was sitting there. Maybe he's in the can. Oh well. Anyway, this is the dude I'm always talking about—he was our QB on that championship team I was on . . ."

Billy grabs the handle to the men's room, pausing as he whips his head toward the bar. No one is watching. He slips out the back, hugging the wall until he gets to the corner. Cautious, he peeks, checking that no one is waiting to pounce. *It looks clear.* He dashes to his truck. He gives a visual sweep before climbing in and firing up the engine. *Damn, maybe Brett's, right? Maybe I should leave. But where would I go? It doesn't matter. Drive.*

Six

Do Ya Feel Me?

Julian rushes down the hall; the captain has requested his presence. He enters the captain's office. The FBI agents sit on the far side of the room. Julian freezes.

The captain barks, "Get your ass in here."

"Sorry," Julian replies, eyeing the agents.

"Where's Perez?"

"He's working another drive-by."

"Well, hell. Okay, I guess you'll do," the captain says. "These are the FBI agents, ahh Hanks and—"

"Broadway," Veronica says, rising, offering her hand. They exchange handshakes.

"They're working the hostel shooting," the captain says. "They have some questions."

I have some questions for them, Julian thinks. "How can I help?" Julian asks, folding his arms, leaning against the captain's desk.

"We're at a dead-end," Walter remarks. "We were thinking—"

"This William Bates—" Veronica says.

"Uh-huh," Julian remarks.

"Did you ever find a connection between him and the victim?"

"Nothing. The closest I was able to come up with was some coin-toss event that happened in Texas."

Veronica opens her notebook. "At The Truck Stop in Water Valley."

"That would be the one."

"That coach died there? Right?"

"The coach died here in Chicago."

"Right. He was the assistant coach. We're talking about the head coach, Thompson."

"I don't know about him. I was focused on the victim and Billy. Sorry, William. The head coach died?"

"Kinda."

"Kinda?" He chuckles. "What does that mean?"

"I guess he came back to life, or something," Veronica says. "Like a resurrection."

"Like what—a near-death thing?"

"No. The report is he died—I guess for a while. He was in the morgue when they found him, alive."

"You're shitting me?" Julian glances at the captain, snickering. "Wow."

"That's the report we have."

"Interesting."

"Very. I'm guessing you never interviewed the coach, his wife, or the father-in-law?" Walter asks.

"No, that never came up. I just got the report that he shot up some people down in Mooresville—stole a few cars and ended up here in Chicago."

"Did you recover the car he drove here in?"

"When he checked in, he didn't put down a vehicle. We're waiting for an abandoned vehicle, but so far, nothing has popped up."

"We got this report from the Texas Rangers. The victim did go on the shooting spree and put Thompson's wife in the hospital."

"Right. You think one of them went after the victim?"

"It's a thread we were chasing. It seems they all have alibis," Walter says. "Which is why we're at a dead-end."

"I never talked to any of them. But it seems reasonable one of them would have shot the victim. Like I say, they all had alibis."

"Thank you, officer," Veronica says, standing.

"Excuse me, before you go. Did you interview any of them?" Julian asks.

"Not the wife, but we did talk to the coach and the wife's father."

"Anything interesting?"

"They both wanted him dead. He did almost kill the wife, after all. And we did think we had something. The father-in-law was in the Marines—he's an excellent marksman, but as far as we could trace, he was in Mooresville at the time of the shooting here in Chicago." Veronica says. "So—"

"I see that look in your eye," Walter remarks. "We thought the same thing. We checked him out. He was an admin clerk in the Marines. He did have a few pistols, but the trail died there."

"Did you get a look at his cache?" Julian asks.

"Yeah. He has a couple of nine millimeters and two forty-fives."

"No rifles?"

"Not that we saw. Of course, we didn't serve him and do a raid."

"When did he serve?" Julian asks. Walter looks at Veronica. She refers to her notes.

"Ah, he was in Vietnam sixty-six to sixty-nine."

"Anything else?" Walter asks. Julian shakes his head. "Thank you, detective." The two agents clear the room.

"Okay, Julian, what's going on in the that head of yours?"

Julian glances at the captain. "Oh, nothing."

"Yeah, right."

Lounging poolside, Tom reflects that it was seven short hours ago he was in the frigid cold of Cleveland. Now, he basks in the warmth of this tropical island. He also basks in the peace; when's the last time he could breathe and relax? It's been a long time. He sips a drink.

"What is this?" Tom asks.

"A mai tai," Ann replies.

Tom takes another swig. "I really like this."

"I thought you might."

"I can't believe all the things I've missed out on before I met you."

"There's a lot in the world to experience."

"I'm seeing that. I guess I've been too focused on one thing—anyway, I could get to liking this life a lot."

"Honey, this is your life."

Tom cocks his head. "Yeah, I guess so."

Ann observes a group gathering at the poolside bar. They're pointing at Tom.

"Oh no."

"What?"

"A storm is coming."

Tom tilts his head to the sky. "What are you talking about? It's clear. God, it's beautiful here."

"I think we're about to have company."

The group watches in anticipation as a lady approaches.

"Excuse me, sir."

Tom gazes into her eyes. "Yes."

"You're him, aren't you?"

"I don't know. Who are you looking for?"

"The coach. You're that coach—right?"

Tom looks behind her, seeing the others follow her lead like ants heading to a picnic. Tom locks eyes with Ann, who shrugs.

Tom looks at the woman. "I guess you got me. How can I help you?"

"Would you sign this for me?" She shoves a pad with a pen at him.

"Ah, sure." Scribbling his signature.

"Thank you." Tom smiles. "I just want you to know I'm a fan." She scurries off.

Looking at Ann, he says, "Wow, even here."

"I told you. It's like you're Elvis."

Turning back, a woman stands with a small child. "Excuse me, sir, we were all talking over there. Are you him? You're him, right?"

"I guess the word is out. Yes, I'm him."

"I was wondering if you could bless my child?"

Tom glances behind her at the quickly forming line. "What?"

"My child, could you bless my child?"

"I'm sorry, I don't bless things—or people, sorry."

"I have money. I'll pay you."

"You want to pay me?"

"Yes."

"I don't want your money. Really, I don't do blessings." The lady scowls, stomping away. A large burly man is next.

"Sorry to bother you, sir, but could you sign this?" Tom sighs. "Also, I was wondering, could you advise me where to invest my money? Do you see any good investments coming up within the next six months or so?"

"Sorry, I think you really need a financial adviser for that. I don't do that sort of thing."

"Isn't that a shame—okay. Thanks for the autograph."

Next is a woman carrying a baby. "Oh sir, I was wondering, could you bless my child?"

"I'm sorry, I don't bless people—or things—"

"It's time to go," Ann proclaims, standing. "Sorry, we have an appointment." Tom nods to Ann. He joins her. The crowd moans. The chatter increases as Tom waves, and they slink off.

Ann flicks her phone open. "Hi, we need a car. Something small. And book us into that spot on the other side of the island . . . That's the one."

In a low voice, Tom asks, "Are they following us?"

Ann glances over her shoulder. "Uh-huh."

"Damn. Where do we go?"

"Anywhere but our room."

"This part sucks. What's with the blessing stuff?"

"I don't know. I guess they think you have special powers?"

"I do? I mean, my vision is better, but I can't see through walls. I have better feeling in my hands, but what can you do with that?"

"Bless people." They laugh. "The word is you did that miracle on your wife."

"Oh shit, I forgot about that one." They walk faster. "I guess people are pretty gullible sometimes?"

"You have no idea—here, this looks good," Ann tugs Tom's arm, steering him into a conference room. She glances over her shoulder. "They're not following."

"Jesus."

"Yeah, I get the feeling they think you're him." They chuckle. Ann's eyes circle the room—they're alone. She smiles. Tom gazes into Ann's eyes, drawing her into an embrace—they kiss.

"Oh boy, we need to get to the room." Tom nods.

FBI agents weren't honest with Julian. The Texas Rangers had given them another name. They wanted to know if Julian had come across it. Julian didn't say anything; they wondered if he was keeping Skinny to himself. They migrated south to this Texas creek, looking at this mobile home. Walter is agitated as it wasn't a fun trip to get here. A dust cloud drifts, collecting on the agents as they stand looking at a mobile home. Veronica fans the air, coughing.

"Sure, is dusty," She remarks.

"Uh-huh, driving on dirt roads will do that," Walter remarks, peeking into a window. "I don't think anyone is home."

"Because there's not a vehicle?"

"Yep." Walter bangs on the door. "Plus, it's too quiet."

Veronica gazes at the tall trees and listens to the sound of the creek. "Kind of a nice setting."

"If you like pover—" The door opens. A long-legged blonde woman stands, looking annoyed. "Hello, ma'am," Walter says, showing his badge. "We're with the FBI. Can we talk to Theodore Hart?"

"FBI. Jesus. What did he do?"

"We just wanted to have a chat."

"A chat? The FBI wants to have a chat? I'm sure you do."

"Ahh, yes, ma'am."

Tracy smiles. "He's not here. He's been gone for a couple of days—he does that."

"Do you know where he went? Or where we could find him?"

"I don't know—he's most likely drinkin', and God knows what else?"

"I see. Do you know anything about him taking a trip to Chicago lately?"

"He doesn't tell me shit. He hasn't been around much lately."

"Are you two married?"

"God no. We cohabitate."

"I see. Any word when he'll be back?"

"No . . . But I'm sure he'll blow back through sometime. Ya wanna wait?"

Walter eyes Veronica. She raises an eyebrow.

"How long would that be?"

"I have no idea. It could be days."

"I see. Is there a bar or honky-tonk he likes to go to around here?"

"This is a dry County. You'll have to go to Midland."

"Dry County—I haven't heard that one in a while. Where in Midland? You know, to narrow the search."

"You could try The Blue Door or The Bar."

"The Bar?" Walter asks. Tracy nods. "There's a place called, The Bar?"

"Yep. Or the Blue Door. Good luck."

Skinny crouches behind a big bush, spying on Billy's house. Well, he thinks it's Billy's house. Aaron gave him directions after the fourth shot of tequila. It was one too many drinks, or maybe two too many. He pulls the napkin out, reading for the seventh time. Arron wrote go down past the rose bush with a bunch of squiggly lines that was supposed to be a map. *You make one fucked up map, Aaron.* He stuffs the napkin into his back pocket. He sways from too much tequila. *Man, I'm still pretty fucked up. Maybe this isn't such a good idea. Maybe I should come back when I sober up some more—when I'm thinkin' better.*

He gets distracted. *Boy, that dude sure has a big porch.* Big indeed. The porch covers the front of the house, wrapping around the left side. *You could have a kegger on a porch like that.*

He glances at his watch. *It sure is quiet. What does this guy drive?* There are no vehicles parked in the driveway. *I'll bet he drives a truck. Maybe there's something parked in that garage?* Off to the left, there's a detached triple car garage. *Fuck, I should get a garage. And this motherfucker has a three-car garage.*

He glances at his watch, calculating, or trying to calculate, how long he's been behind the bush. *Fuck, man, I can't stay here forever. Here goes nothing.* He emerges with a steady pace. His adrenaline is flowing, heightening his senses, which helps to clear his head. He can feel his heartbeat. There's something exhilarating about doing shit like this. Getting closer to the house, a TV is playing. *I had a feeling he was here.*

Scaling the steps, a board creaks; it's so loud, or so it seems. *Ah, shit.* He freezes, tensing up. He waits, watches, listens. *They probably can't hear that over the TV.* The big picture window catches his fancy; he watches for the curtains to move. All is calm. Relief flushes through his body. He relaxes. He continues with softer steps, reaching the big picture window. Peeking through a slit in the curtains, it's dark. The only light illuminating the room is coming from the TV. His head whips in both directions. Zoning in on the front door, he shuffles over, giving it a light rap. Nothing. He knocks again, harder. *What, they left the TV on?* He twists back to the big picture window. Getting more aggressive, he cups his hands, pressing his face against his hands; his nose is against the window. *Damn, I can't see shit.* He returns to the front door, twisting the knob—it doesn't give. He gives more pressure—it's locked. *Who locks their front door in the middle of the day?*

Standing back, he studies the porch, which is calling—*follow me.* He takes the bait, following the porch around the side of the house. *Wow, this thing wraps all the way to the back?* Crouching, he hugs the wall. He comes to another window. Sneaking a peek, there's not even a slit to look through. *Doesn't this fuckin' guy like sunlight? What is he, a vampire?*

He pushes to the corner. Pausing, he presses his back to the wall. Taking a breath, he cranes his head around the corner, peeking. A closed umbrella is planted in the middle of a table with chairs, and a barbecue, looking lonely. With soft steps, he eases his way to the sliding glass door—it's open. A drape flaps in the breeze. *What the? The TV is on, the front is locked, and the sliding glass door is open. What's wrong with this picture?* He contemplates. *Ya know someone is waiting. Dude, you should leave now.* He checks for his ice pick. *This thing isn't going to help if they got a gun, which they probably do.* He can't help himself, like a moth to the flame. He inches closer, straining to see inside. He sees the countertop and stove. *Okay, it's now or never.* He makes his move, stepping over the threshold, planting one foot inside the house—there's an awful sound—he knows that sound—it's a shotgun being racked. His head snaps toward the sound—Peggy sits in a chair with a shotgun at the ready. *Oh fuck.*

"Who the hell are you?" she barks.

Skinny raises his arms, backing up. "Ah, ah, um, I'm Burt."

"Uh-huh. Like in Burt and Ernie?"

"Ah, I guess?" Skinny shuffles backward with little steps so small it doesn't look like he's moving as he inches toward the edge of the deck.

"What the hell ya doing sneakin' around the house?"

"I was looking for Billy. Ah, ah, um, we work together. Can ya put the shotgun down?" If he inches any closer to the edge of the deck, he'll tumble off.

"I don't think I'm done using it?"

"Oh shit. That's what—" Skinny jumps, somersaulting down the hill. Peggy fires, missing. Skinny pops up like a little critter. She fires the second chamber, catching Skinny's left shoulder. *Shit! Damn, that fuckin' stings. Fuck, fuck, fuck.* Skinny flexes and rotates the arm as he runs; he's not waiting for her to reload. Scampering in a zigzag pattern, he's a tough target. Peggy is slow reloading; she's not quick like when she was a hell-raiser, back when she wore a younger hairstyle. She doesn't see or move well. Planting her feet, she raises the barrel. She's lost him. A bush moves, or so she thinks—she shoots.

"Shit. I lost the son of a bitch."

The blood dribbles down Skinny's shoulder, dripping on his armrest and the leather seat. When he left Billy's, his arm screamed with pain but since then it's gone numb. Focusing on driving helps to take his mind off the throbbing, but this is the longest drive home ever. There have been moments where he thought he would pass out, but between the throbbing shoulder, the adrenaline pumping, and his active mind, he's alert.

What the hell was I thinking? I know better. Shit. Fuck, I shouldn't have gone there drunk. I knew I shouldn't have stepped into the house. What an idiot. I'm lucky she missed the first shot—she probably would have killed me. Visions of lying dead off the back of Billy's deck evade his thoughts. He shivers. *Okay, quit thinking about that shit.* The thought is not easy to shake. He finds another thought to sink his teeth into. *Sometimes, you're not too bright. Who else would do something that stupid? No one, just you, you stupid piece of shit.* He focuses on driving and pushing the piss-yellow Caddy down the dirt road—he's almost home.

He's to the spot in the road where there's a dip—a big dip—so easy to bottom out a vehicle. To add to the fun, it also curves in front of a huge oak tree that sits guard. The oak is scared from the many who have wandered the road late at night planting their vehicle into the trunk. It's happened so many times over the years, it's amazing the tree is standing. There have been times, late at night, with a few too many drinks, that he's planted a vehicle or two into the tree.

Traveling faster than normal, he hits the dip—the G-force has his stomach is in his throat. The dirt gives way—the car slides. Fighting to keep the car out of the oak, the tires grab just enough that he misses the oak by inches. *Man, that was too close.* Now, it's a straight shot to his mobile home.

He stomps on the brakes; the tires grind, spitting rock and pebbles, creating swallow trench in the gravel as the Caddy skids to a stop. Out of habit, he hits the latch and lunges his bad shoulder into the car door. *FUCK.* He grimaces, grabbing his shoulder; he's torn the wound enough to create a new river of blood. *FUCK, FUCK.* He dances a bit. He throws his hip into the door, slamming it shut. Darting to the front door, he stumbles but stays upright—he hasn't moved this fast in years. Bursting through the door, he trips, sliding on the kitchen floor; he tucks, landing on his good arm. Tracy lounges on the couch, watching TV. She pops up like a prairie dog. He is hidden from view behind the kitchen counter.

"Skinny, Skinny." She races to the kitchen. He comes into view—her mouth drops. "What the fuck? What did you do?"

He rocks clutching his arm. "This fuckin' old lady shot me."

She laughs. "Yeah, right."

"It's not funny. She could have killed me."

"What?" Blood is collecting on the floor. She bends down. "What old lady?"

"I don't know." He laughs. "She really fucked me up."

"Shit, you're a fuckin' mess." She darts to the closet, snatching the first aid kit.

"Ya, think I don't know that?"

Tracy rushes back. "I told you before, don't fuck with old ladies. Dammit, Skinny—what are ya doing?" Popping the lid, the contents tumble to the floor, scattering a mosaic of Band-Aids, gauze, white tape, and ointment packets. "Dammit."

"Easy, girl."

She returns a strained smile as she scrambles to collect only what she thinks she needs. She pauses, gazing at the wound.

"I think I'm going to have to cut your shirt."

"Fuck the shirt. Cut it."

She takes the scissors, slicing off a square piece of material. Holding the material up, she peeps through the holes.

"Look at that, it's a bloody piece of Swiss cheese." She flings the material. She works quickly. "Christ, this is bad." Skinny nods. "What, old lady? Why'd she shoot you? Fuck, I can't stop the blood." In one fluid motion, she rises, snatching the paper towels roll from the counter, tearing off a few sheets, slapping them on the wound.

Skinny laughs. "She shot again but missed—I was too fast."

"What the hell ya laughing for? Sounds like you're lucky she didn't kill ya." She tosses the blood-soaked towels into the sink. Ripping fresh paper towels from the roll, she presses on the new ones on the wound. "Did you roll in the dirt?"

He nods "It was the only way to escape."

She works the paper towel. "It looks like ya still got buckshot in there. I think ya need to go to the hospital."

"Take 'em out."

"What?"

"Aren't there tweezers in that little kit? Throw some coke on it."

"You really want me probing around in your shoulder?"

"Yeah. I trust you. Go ahead. Get some coke. I'll be okay."

"What are you into?" Skinny returns a dead-eyed stare. "Dude, what is going on with you? The FBI was here."

"The FBI? Shit."

"Yeah, that got your attention. First the Rangers, and now the FBI."

"What did they want?"

"They were asking about a trip to Chicago?"

"Fuck—how did they find out about that? Shit. It's that Billy."

"So, ya went?"

"Yeah. I took Pete. I was at the guy's house that ran him over, and I think his mom is the one that shot me."

"Great, you're out there settling a score? Starting a little war? Should I go stay somewhere else for a while?"

"Maybe . . . Shit, I don't know? I'm havin' a hard time finding the motherfucker. First, fix my arm before I bleed out here on the kitchen floor."

She rises, going to the closet. "I don't know about this—you should go to the hospital." She brings back a baggy. Dusting the wound with the white powder, she waits for it to take effect. "Does Brett have anything to do with all of this?"

"What ya talkin' about?"

"My mom called, saying he was in the hospital. Something about his leg."

Skinny smiles.

Seven

Welcome Back, My Friends, to the Show That Never Ends

Kathy is planted in a chair, watching Tom on Oprah. She's finally out of the hospital, so there's comfort in that. As she watches Tom, she's trying to reconcile the story; after all, it's her story. The gravity of Tom's journey has eluded her until now. She's gone through a lot, but Tom's life has been turned inside out. *I guess we're both lucky to be alive.* She never had a full recounting of the beating he took that led to his death. And now, he's being interviewed by Oprah. *Oprah, Jesus. He's a damn rock star.* Fred enters, handing her a post-it note, which she grabs with her working hand.

"How's he doing?" Fred sits next to her.

In a raspy voice, she says, "I don't know. Good, I guess?" Her voice hasn't recovered from the tubes jammed down her throat during her hospital stay. "What's this?"

"My new phone number."

"New?"

"People keep calling for Tom, so I got a new number. I don't know how long this will last before someone figures it out, but it will bring a little peace for now," Fred says. "It's so good to have you home, sweetie."

"I'm glad to be here. It's nice to be out of that hospital bed. Do you know what happened to Tom, I mean, the whole story?"

"Yeah, he told me. We had a lot of time while waiting for word on you."

"Jesus, that must have been awful. I can only imagine if it was you or one of the kids."

"I've certainly had better moments in my life."

"There's this video floating around where one of Tom's people said he performed a miracle on me. Did he?"

"Hell, I don't know. It was bad, real bad. I thought you were going to die, but here you are, so what difference does it make? Miracle, no miracle, I give thanks you're here."

"Thanks, Dad . . . And Pete was run over?"

"Oh, him. Yeah, in Chicago."

"Good! I'm glad that son of a bitch is dead."

"Now, be careful where you say that."

"I know. I've always hated that man."

"You don't have to worry about that anymore."

"When's the last time Tom was here?"

"It's been a while."

"He's running around with that bitch—"

"Now honey—"

"I know, I know. Running around with that nurse."

"Yeah. We had a situation here, and he took off—it was like he was a magnet, and he sucked all the media people with him—it was like vacuumed the street clean."

"They were here?"

"The street was filled with them—it was a Goddamn circus."

"Sounds like the hospital in Texas."

"I don't know about that. I keep waiting for one of his groupies to show up."

"They were here too?"

"Oh yeah." The doorbell rings. Fred looks at his watch. "Who the—God, I hope it's not one of them."

"I think it's Cindy?"

"Cindy? Cindy from Texas, Cindy?"

"Uh-huh. I told you, didn't I?"

"No."

"I thought I did?"

"Is she staying?"

"Yeah, for a few days. I didn't tell you?"

"Not that I remember, but maybe I've got a memory issue."

"No, it's probably me. I seem to be forgetting things lately."

"Okay, I'll get a room ready." He peeks through the peephole. "I don't see anyone."

"She's not the largest person in the world."

Fred turns on the porch light, taking another peek; it's a large black man.

Fred mumbles, "What the hell?" He doesn't open the door. He yells, "Who are you? And what do you want?"

"I'm Julian Thayer." He shows his badge. "Can you see this?"

"Yeah, yeah. What do you want?"

"I'm a police officer from Chicago."

He mumbles, "Chicago? Fuck."

"Yes. I'm looking to talk to Fred Winters."

Chicago? Fuck, fuck. Fred's mind races. *He's here to arrest me. No, he's from Chicago, it's not his jurisdiction, but it is murder. Wouldn't he have a boatload of police with him if he was here to arrest me? They'd probably bust the door down.*

"Dad, are you okay?"

"I'm not sure." He goes back to yelling. "Are you with anyone?"

"No, it's just me."

"Well, stand aside so I can see." Fred cracks the door. "From where?"

"Chicago."

"What's a police officer from Chicago doing here?"

"Sorry for the late call. I'm here on unofficial business."

"Unofficial? Sounds bad. Let me see your badge again." Julian slides his badge through the crack to Fred.

"Can I come in for a minute? It's cold out here."

"Okay." Fred widens the door, letting Julian in. Julian and Kathy's eyes lock. "This is my daughter—"

"Mrs. Thompson?"

"You know me?"

"Not really. I've been working on the Pete Russ case, and you came up, you know, with the shooting. When did you get home?"

Oh, shit, the Pete Russ case. Fuck, I shouldn't have let him in. Don't panic, let's see what the man wants.

"They released me yesterday."

"Good to hear. I understand you went through quite an ordeal—"

"She's damn lucky to be alive," Fred remarks.

"I can see that. How are you feeling these days?"

"Thank God I can walk, but I can't use my left arm. I guess I'm lucky he shot up my left shoulder. Although, I don't feel lucky."

"She was really close to dying," Fred adds.

Julian nods. "Pete Russ did this to you?"

"Yeah, that ass—I mean, yes."

"He shot at all of us; it's Kathy that was the unlucky one," Fred says. "Is that why you're here?"

"Ah, yes. The FBI let me know I should have interviewed a few other people—you know, to try to get a fix on what Pete Russ was doing in Chicago."

"Have a seat," Fred says. "Would you like something? Water, Coke? I know it's late, but coffee, maybe?"

"Nah, no, thank you, I'm good." Julian sits on the couch across from Kathy. "Is your husband here?"

Kathy points. "He's on Oprah."

"What?" Julian twists to see the TV. "Oprah."

"Yeah, he's quite the celebrity these days," Kathy remarks.

"Oprah. Wow." Julian turns his attention back to Kathy. The doorbell rings. Julian looks at his watch. "Busy place."

"You have no idea," Fred remarks, moving to the peephole. He opens the door. "I hope you're Cindy?"

"Mr. Winters?"

"Yep."

"Hi, I'm Cindy Willetts. It's so nice to finally meet you."

"You too. Come on out of the cold. Kathy's been waiting for you." Fred's not sure if he should hug her or shake her hand. Cindy offers her hand. Julian gives her pause, but she turns her attention to Kathy.

"Oh, girlfriend, it's so good to see you," Kathy says.

"Oh, you too." Cindy moves in for a hug.

"Easy, easy. The shoulder."

Cindy pulls back. "Of course. Is that what that asshole did to you?"

Julian raises a brow.

"Yeah, yeah. It was raining glass."

"You were shot too, right, Mr. Winters?" Cindy asks.

"Yeah. The bullets were flying everywhere. And call me Fred."

"I'm so glad that asshole is dead," Cindy remarks.

Fred clears his throat. "Cindy, this is officer?"

"Thayer."

"Yes, Thayer. He's from Chicago."

Cindy turns to him. "Oh my. Chicago." Julian nods. "Do you know about what happened to Pete Russ?"

"Yes. I'm doing some follow-up investigation."

"And I'm interrupting."

"No, no," Fred says. "You're fine."

"Maybe you can help. Did you know Pete Russ?" Julian asks.

"Did I. What a waste—" Cindy stops.

"It's okay," Julian says. "I would like to hear a take on someone who knew him. Did you know him well?"

"I've known Pete since he was a boy."

"A boy—really."

"Yeah. Such a cute little boy. But he didn't age well. He got hooked up with that Skinny Hart, and let's just say, it was a bad mix."

"You don't say," Julian replies, pulling out his notebook. "Have you got any idea why Pete would go postal on these fine people?"

"I don't have a clue. If I were to guess, I'd say Burt and Skinny are at the root of it."

"Burt?" Julian asks. "You're saying names that I haven't heard before."

"Oh, he's the barber in town."

"This is in—"

"Big Springs. It's a small town in Texas. It's by Midland. Most folks know Midland."

"Ahh, Big Springs. This barber, Burt, he's powerful?"

"Pretty much runs everything. At least he thinks he does. He uses Skinny to do the dirty work, if ya know what I mean?"

"I do." Julian wonders why this woman couldn't have popped up on his radar earlier. He's not going to let this one go until he squeezes this lemon dry. "Do you know William Bates? I guess he goes by Billy?"

"Who? No, I don't know that name."

"He's the one that ran over Pete," Fred remarks.

"Oh, him. I'd sure like to give that boy a medal." Cindy turns to Kathy. "Look what Pete did to you."

"Did Billy hang out in Big Springs?"

"Not that I know."

"Tell me more about this Burt."

"He's this old guy. He's been the barber in Big Springs forever. He's always trying to fix things. Word has it he cooked up a plan to keep Pete out of jail."

"Pete was going to jail?" Julian asks.

Cindy turns to Kathy. "Do you want to explain?"

"No, you're doing great."

"Let's just say they were trying to chase the Thompsons out of town, and things got real ugly."

"And it worked?"

"Not really. Tom wouldn't go."

Julian locks eyes with Kathy. "Did you leave?"

"Yeah, but Tom wouldn't go. He said he had a contract to teach."

"But he was the football coach."

"It's all the same thing."

"Huh."

"I'll bet you have gotten more than you thought you would," Fred remarks.

Julian nods. "About this Skinny..."

Julian is brought up to speed on Skinny, Kathy, Tom, Ann, the reporters, Burt, and Pete for the next hour. He writes some of it down, but mainly he listens.

"Wow," Julian says. "This all sounds like it would make a great movie. You certainly have been through a lot, Mrs. Thompson."

"I appreciate that. It's nice someone outside of my friends and family has noticed."

"I can certainly see why you all have strong feelings about Pete Russ."

"Yeah, well."

Julian looks at Fred. He looks at Kathy and Cindy visiting. He looks at Fred again. Fred smiles, watching Cindy and Kathy. It's the first time Fred has seen Kathy smile since she got out of the hospital.

Julian excuses himself. Stepping onto the porch, Julian pauses, reflecting. Kathy and Cindy threw off his timing. Seeing Kathy causes a stir within him. *Damn, what would I do if she were my daughter?* He's always trying to stay neutral. *Man, that Cindy was sure helpful.* He was here to question Fred. He ponders going back inside. *Another time.* Julian heads to his car—he's got other things to investigate.

Eight

High Noon

Lester and his crew surround Tom and Ann, leading them through the maze of hallways in the belly of the New York studio.

"Lester, are we going the right way?" Tom asks.

"Yes, I did a pre-run—we're almost out."

Emerging from the New York studio, a large crowd is waiting.

"Oh boy," Ann remarks.

The chatter is immediate as the noise swells. The crowd rushes, swallowing up Tom's group; the pushing and shoving begins. Lester's crew pushes, but it's slow going. They plow toward the waiting limousine. A crew member falls; Tom helps him up. A woman breaks through, rushing Tom with a Sharpie and pad of paper—Tom signs. The crew restores the buffer; the woman is ecstatic to be inside the circle. The chauffeur waits with the car door open, ready to sweep them away to their hotel. Ann ducks into the car first—Tom follows. The woman, thinking she part of the gang, tries to follow Tom into the limo; a crew member grabs her arm, yanking her back—the door slams shut.

"Are you okay?" Tom asks.

"I'm fine," Ann remarks. "Wow, it seems like you're getting more famous."

"Isn't that great? I need a vacation—from them."

"That may be true, but I don't think they're going away."

"What if I do? Won't that kill it?"

"What? Going away? Like, what, disappearing?"

"Yeah."

"Ordinarily, I'd say yes, but this is like a religion," Ann remarks. "They think you're the one."

"I thought that going on Oprah tonight would help this die down."

"Give it some time. The fever may break. But you need to operate like it won't. It would help if you had some protocols. And we need to start using back entrances."

"Isn't that what we just did?"

"Yeah, I guess."

"It seems I can't go out anymore. How do all these people know who I am?"

"That's a silly question."

"Yeah, I guess?"

"Look, all huge celebrities deal with this all the time."

"Great."

"Giving them a way to approach you—contact you. Something more controlled."

"Like what?"

"You should have events, charge money. And definitely get professional security."

"What? Charge money? They already give me money."

"They'll give you *more* money."

"They will? I just want to coach football."

"I think that ship has sailed."

Skinny plants himself on a bar stool at The Cue Ball. Tim tends the bar.

"What can I get for ya?" Tim asks.

"Whiskey, neat."

"Any particular kind?"

"Surprise me."

"Okay." Tim grabs a bottle and glass, setting them in front of Skinny. "I've seen you in here before, right?"

"Right. I was with Aaron—the other day."

"That's right. You guys were sitting over in the corner. Weren't you guys drinking tequila?"

"Very good. I like switching things up."

"Oh. How do ya know Aaron?"

"We were on the championship football team together."

"What's your name?"

"Skinny."

"Skinny . . . Oh shit, you're that Skinny?"

"I don't know. It depends on what we're talkin' about?"

"He's always going on and on about that team and the quarterback, Skinny."

"That would be me."

"I'll be. He always goes on about how cool you were under pressure."

"That's what they tell me . . . Say, I was in here lookin' for Billy, ya know where I can find him?"

"Home, maybe?"

"I tried there."

"Do ya know Sylvia?"

"Nah."

"He might be there. But to tell you the truth, the boy hasn't been right since Little John died."

"Little John?"

"Yeah, the guy who killed that coach—from Big Springs? I guess the coach didn't actually die, so it would be more accurate to say he put him in the hospital. Bottom line, he beat the crap out of him."

"He was friends with him?"

"Yep."

"And he was from here?"

"Yep."

Skinny crunches the flow chart in his head. Pete tells Little John that the coach was breaking into his truck, the coach goes to the hospital, Little John dies, and then Billy runs over Pete. *Interesting. It looks like things are coming into focus. So, if this Billy knew about Pete, Brett must have told him everything. Did that son of a bitch track me to Chicago? Damn, that's it, isn't it? Fuckin' Brett. So, are Brett and Billy working together? That would make sense—yeah, they're working together. That fuckin' weasel. I'm going to make your ass pay—after I take care of that Billy. I gotta watch out for that Billy, he likes to run people over.*

"Where does Sylvia live?" Skinny asks.

"You serious?"

"Yeah, man."

"I'm not telling ya that."

"How about a twenty." Skinny is holding a twenty-dollar bill.

"What? No way, man." Tim starts wiping the counter. "I think it's time you left."

Skinny switches bills, slapping it on the bar. "A hundred?"

Tim stares at the bill, thinking, *What's this dude doing with a hundred dollars?*

"How about two hundred?"

Tim's palms sweat. That's a lot of money in a place like Sterling City.

Skinny smiles as he reads the post-it note. *Everybody's got a price.* He reviews the address: *514 Hiler Ave. Where the fuck is this place?* He's going in circles. Washington Street to 1st Street, and back to Main Street—he's done this three times. He stops at the corner of Main and 1st. *What the fuck? He told me this was on the south edge of town. Okay, slow down, dude.* He studies the post-it note again. Raising his head, his eyes lock on it—there it is—a small sign: Hiler Avenue. *What the fuck?*

Main Street becomes Hiler? Who designed this fucking place? Putting the car in gear, he creeps onto Hiler. It's a small street that curves, winding back to Washington Street. He follows the bend, and there it is: 514 Hiler. He eases the Caddy onto a gravel patch in front of Sylvia's house. There's a small sidewalk a tad larger than a car, and a walkway that leads to the front porch. *No driveway?* There is a dirt road on the edge of the property, but it's hard to tell if it's a road or a driveway. *Is that their driveway?* There are no cars or trucks parked out front. He gives a visual sweep of the area. *Man, this is kind of isolated.* There's only one other house across the street.

Hearing the car tires crushing the gravel out front, Billy pops up, stealing a peek through the window.

"Is someone here?" Sylvia asks.

"Shit."

"What?"

"It's that piss-yellow Caddy," Billy remarks. Sylvia moves to take a peek. "No, no, stay down. I need to get out of here. Stall him as long as you can."

"What are you talking about?"

"I'll explain later—stall him."

Billy darts out the back. There's a knock at the door.

Sylvia yells, "Who are you? And why shouldn't I shoot your ass?"

"Don't shoot," Skinny says, raising his arms; he doesn't want to go through that again. "I'm looking for Billy. I was told you might—" He whips his head toward a roaring engine and a truck racing on the edge of the property. *Is that him?* Skinny squints. *Crap, he's making a run for it.*

The truck slides sideways onto Hiler. Billy plunges the pedal to the floor. The tires break loose, spitting gravel, pelting the Caddy's front end; it sounds like machine gunfire. Billy glances through the rearview mirror at the Caddy taking fire—smirking. *Take that, you piece of shit.* At Washington Street, Billy takes a hard left and is gone.

"Fuck." Skinny flies off the porch. He jumps, sliding over the hood of the Caddy like a stuntman; he's not ready for the gravel landing. He slips, crashing to the ground on his left side, landing on his hip and his bad shoulder. "Fuck." With his adrenaline pumping, he doesn't pay attention to the pain; he doesn't take time to dust himself off as he climbs into his Caddy, giving chase.

Billy has a sizable lead, but Skinny spots a rooster tail of dust—this is where the Caddy shines—power. He closes the gap—kind of. Billy is on a backcountry road, thinking he has the advantage. But, Skinny grew up driving on dirt roads; he pushes the Caddy, closing the gap. Billy eyes the rearview mirror. *Shit.* Skinny is making up ground. Billy down shifts, pushing the truck even harder.

Cresting a big hill, the truck takes air, landing with a thud—testing the suspension. The truck catapults back into the air. Billy's head hits the roof—he hears a crack. *Was that my neck?* His ears ring. The top of his head stings—a new knot is born. The pain is a mild distraction as the adrenaline pulses through his body; his attention is on bringing the wild beast that has become his truck under control. There's a curve to negotiate. He ignores it. *Time to go cross country.* The terrain is rough; the truck bounces about as it hits rocks and holes. Billy feels like he's riding a bucking bronco. *No way that piss-yellow Caddy can follow me over this shit.*

Skinny's turn. His Caddy launches—he can't see land. *Oh shit.* The Caddy nose dives, plowing a crater in the dirt road—smack—Skinny plants his face into the steering wheel—he sees stars. The back-end crashes back to earth. The Caddy looks like it is stuck in a snowdrift, except it's a drift of dirt. There's a knot on his forehead. *Fuck!* He's foggy. He's trying to grasp the situation. *Who hit me?* He thinks he has taken a big hit in a football game. His vision is wonky. He's looking for the grass and the guy who hit him. *Who hit me? What's going on? Where's the coach? The crowd? The scoreboard? My teammates?* The billowing black smoke from the engine serves as smelling salts—he coughs. The fog is lifting. As the seconds tick, things become clearer. *My car. Shit! What did I do to my car?* He gazes at the black plumes of smoke rising from the hood. *Fuck, my car is on fire? Fire! Shit!* He launches his bad shoulder into the car door, jarring the door open. *Fuck!* The pain shoots through his body. His knees are weak as he wobbles, falling to the ground. *What the*—A loud crunching metal sound gets louder; it sounds like the crunching of aluminum cans. He grabs his shoulder. The throbbing from his head begs for attention. He touches the knot on his forehead. *Damn.* He checks his hand for blood—there's blood, not from his head, but from his shoulder. *Shit, my head is bleeding.* He fights to get to his feet, which alerts him to the pain in his hip. He's a mess. *What? How did I hurt my hip? In the car?* He struggles to remember. It's like he's awoken from a dream, and he's trying to put the pieces together.

He studies the car. The smoke is now black vapor. He is in a cloud of burned oil—he coughs. He's in a pattern of pressing the knot on his forehead, pulling his hand down, and examining his hand for blood. Each time he touches his forehead, he paints his face with more blood. *Shit, I'm bleeding. That's bad, isn't it? Head wounds are always bad.* He looks for someplace he might stumble to get help—it's fields in every direction. *Where the fuck am I? How did I get here?* His wounded car is tapping, quivering out one final shake as the engine dies. *Christ, I killed my car.* Giving a visual sweep of the area, he sees fields—not a building in sight. He whips open his cell phone. *Who should I call?* It doesn't matter—there are no bars. *Shit.*

Looking down at the small valley, and up the next hill, he decides to head back over the hill from the direction he came. He limps. His hip is throbbing—his head is throbbing—his shoulder is throbbing. He crests the hill; the town comes into view. *Hallelujah, a town. What town is this?* Like kernels of corn in a popcorn machine, memories pop in: Tim, The Cue Ball, falling on his ass—Billy. *Billy. That's right, I was chasing that asshole.* He looks back toward his car. He can't see it; it's over the crest of the hill. *Wait, I was driving on this road.* He recalls the chase. *He got away. Okay, asshole, I'll give you this round. Things will be different when I get ahold of your ass next time, motherfucker.*

Nine

How Much Longer?

Skinny looks into the mirror. *Jesus, I'm a mess.* He pokes the bump on his forehead. *Well, at least it's not bleeding. I'm going to kill that Billy when I get my hands on him.* The wounds are mounting, which only increases Skinny's lust to catch Billy and settle the score. He pops the Advil, and then washes his face, toweling off. Turning his attention to his shoulder, he rips the badge from his arm. After the wound is cleaned, he slaps a new patch on it.

With his shoulder patched up and his face cleaned, Skinny wanders into the lobby of the auto shop. Grabbing an empty chair, he looks out the big picture window, waiting for the painkillers to kick in—aspirin was all he could get. *I wish I was home so I could get something stronger than aspirin.* He stews. Billy is proving to be slippery. *There must be someone that knows where that asshole went.* A young man with a greasy blue shirt, supporting an embroidered name tag stating *Ned*, approaches.

"Excuse me, is that your Caddy, sir?"

Skinny's head snaps up. "Yeah. And ya don't have to call me sir."

"Sorry. Your oil pan is smashed into the crank. Was it making a tapping noise?"

"Yeah. It sounded like cans being smashed."

"That's why."

"Shit."

"Did you jump it? Like off a ramp or something?"

"Kinda. Damn, anything else?"

"The bumper isn't doing so well, and—"

"And what?"

"The front end has little pits in the paint—"

"It does?"

"Yeah. Was someone throwing rocks at it?"

"Rocks?" Skinny racks his brain.

"Pebbles, maybe. I mean, that's such a nice paint job. Anyway, there's good news—"

"There is?"

"Kinda. The frame on the front end isn't bent. That car is a tough son of a bitch."

"Okay, so what's the damage?"

"We're goin' to have ta straighten the brackets to the bumper, and you'll need a new bumper. Those aren't so easy to get these days for a car like that. We're not sure about the crank, ya know, if ya need a new one, but you'll definitely need a new oil pan. Ya probably know a guy to fix the paint job—ya know, whoever painted originally."

"I do. Okay, how much? How long?"

"I got a guy checkin' on the bumper, so I'm goin' ta guess about three, four days and somewhere north of twenty-five hundred, providing your crank is okay. If we have ta go into the engine, well?"

"Yeah, I get it."

Tom and Ann emerge from the New York hotel; a limousine is waiting with a chauffeur, who is holding the back door open. Lester's crew is on standby. A large crowd also waits; the crowd has been building for hours. Lester's crew snaps into action, creating a cocoon for Tom and Ann. The crowd rushes, swallowing them up, stopping their progress. The pressure builds, Lester's crew struggles to maintain their buffer. The mob has control, pushing them around. Screams rain down. "Tom, Coach, Ann." Because of the competition of getting the couples attention, the crowd intensifies, tightening like an anaconda around its prey, squeezing—the pressure is so great, it's hard to breathe. The crowd pushes Lester's crew back and forth, ebbing and flowing like the ocean waves.

Many wave pens, Sharpies, seeking Tom's autograph. A hand reaches out, snatching Tom's hat. Ann's hat disappears. Like a magic act, Tom's sunglasses vanish. Tom wrestles, trying to keep his right glove. There's a tug on Tom's collar; it rips from his shirt. Ann's sunglasses are snatched from her face, while a lock of her hair is snipped; the trophy is held high in the air as the person dances away. Tom loses the battle for the glove. As the mob moves closer to the limo, the chauffeur is concerned. Like waves crashing on the rocks, the mob slams against the limo, the door slams shut; the chauffeur is pinned against the car. The car shakes like it's in an earthquake. The chauffeur fights to free himself. Tom sets his sights on the limo's door handle. Straining, he stretches out, grabbing the handle, pulling himself closer to the car; he kicks his leg up, planting his foot on the side of the limo, creating leverage to pry the door open; he feels a twinge in his back. *Oh fuck, that's not good.* He latches onto Ann's arm, launching her into the car. He follows; the door shuts like it's vacuum sealed. The driver hits the power locks.

"Oh my God, that was worse than last time," Ann remarks, looking at Tom. He rubs his forehead. "Are you okay?"

"Yeah, I hit my head. Crap, I think a pulled a muscle in my back."

"I thought we were going to die."

"Drive, drive," Tom barks. The crowd rocks the car. The pounding on the car sounds like a hailstorm. The driver eases the car forward, nudging people; a few jump draping themselves on the hood. The driver picks up speed; the yelling and screaming fade; the last of the riders falls to the asphalt, hitting with a nasty slap. Ann plays with her hair.

"Shit, someone cut my hair."

"Damn, I don't want to do that again. Are you okay?"

"I'm alive." Ann glances back. "Do you think Lester's group is okay?"

"Hell, if I know. I'll give him a call in a bit. I thought this would get better after Oprah?"

"We can't do that anymore."

"That's for sure. They ripped my collar off my shirt."

"I see that." No sunglasses, no gloves. Ann smiles. Tom smiles. She pushes the button, closing the window between the driver and them. They kiss.

Skinny scrutinizes each vehicle that passes by; he's getting agitated. *Where is she?* All he wants to do is get out of this hellhole. *Finally.* Tracy pulls up in a truck. Skinny darts out of the waiting room, lunging at the truck's door handle. Getting is open, he pulls himself inside before the truck stops.

He's barking, "Go, go."

"Alright. Chill." Tracy glances in the rearview mirror. "Are you running from someone?"

Skinny is working his shoulder. "Fuck, I think I opened up the wound."

"What the fuck are acting like a monkey for?"

"I just wanted out of there." He's checking the wound. "I guess that wasn't too smart."

"There seems to be a lot of that going on lately."

Skinny grimaces. "Was it hard finding his keys?"

"Nope. Just like you said."

"Good, good."

"What's going on?" Tracy gives a quick glance to Skinny. "What's up with your face?"

He touches the knot. "I fuckin' smacked the steering wheel."

"You what?"

"Ah shit, I really fucked up my car. It's goin' to take a few days for them to fix it."

"What the hell is going on? You come home shot, you've got a fucked-up face, and now you fucked up your car? What's next?"

"The less you know, the better."

"Okay, but we've never had the Rangers and the FBI snooping around. Whatever this is, you need to stop."

"I know, I know. Turn right up here."

"Here?"

"Ya."

"Are you listening to me?"

"Yeah, yeah, I'm listening."

"I thought we'd be goin' back to Big Springs."

"I need to talk with Brett."

"Brett? Why don't ya leave the poor guy alone?"

"He's my conduit."

"Conduit? Conduit to what?"

"Turn here . . . Okay, right here . . . Up on the right, that's his driveway. Okay, I'll be back in a few."

Skinny slithers out of the truck, crossing the street. He moves alongside Brett's house, hugging tight to the garage wall. Tracy watches, trying to figure out what he's up to. *Why the hell isn't he going to the front door?* He disappears through the back gate. He bypasses the garage door, heading for the sliding glass door. Giving the handle a tug, he sighs—it's locked. *Damn. You're getting wiser. I'll give you that.* He raps on the glass. Nothing. He raps again. Brett pulls back the blinds, looking defiant.

"What do you want?" Brett asks.

"Hey, man, let me in."

"I don't think so. What do you want?"

"C'mon man, let me in."

"Not today. What do ya want?"

"Shit. Okay, look, I'm sorry about the ice pick."

"I'll bet you are."

"C'mon man, let me in." Skinny starts banging on the glass. Brett reveals a pistol. Skinny freezes.

"What do you want?"

"Shit. Okay, I almost caught Billy at Sylvia's place; he slipped me. Where do ya think he would go?"

"How do you know where Sylvia lives? I don't even know where she lives."

"I just know, okay? Where do you think he would slither off to?"

"Haven't a clue."

"Shit. Okay. Really, man, I'm sorry about the ice pick."

"Yeah, okay."

They share a stare; Skinny smiles. Brett doesn't.

Skinny is back in the truck.

"What happened?"

"He doesn't know anything."

"Know what?"

"I'm looking for this Billy guy."

"That's what this is all about? Is that how you fucked up your car?"

"Just drive."

Tom takes a break. He's recording his VR presentation—it's not going well. Ann stands, leaning against a table, arms folded, wearing sunglasses; they're working to keep their superpower under control. *I sure am glad she's wearing those sunglasses,* Tom thinks.

"I suck at this," Tom remarks.

"You need to come from the heart."

"I don't know what to say? I've already said it—too many times. Besides, staring into a camera—"

"You never talked to a camera before?"

"I have, but I was always being interviewed."

"So, pretend you're being interviewed. You have lots of new followers that have never heard of this stuff. You were great with Oprah—" Ann's phone rings. "Hello ... Who? ... Right, okay ... how much? ... Okay, I'll let him know and call you back."

"Who was that?"

"60 Minutes—They want to do a piece on you."

"Jesus—60 Minutes. This stuff is not going to stop, is it?"

"That's what I've been trying to tell you."

Lester enters. "Hi Tom, Ann."

"Hi," they echo.

"Okay, I hired some professional bodyguards."

"Good," Tom replies.

"And, Tom, we have to do something with this money."

"The GoFundMe account?"

"Yeah. It's gone ballistic since your appearance on Oprah. It's up to two and a half million."

"What? I'd thought this would all slow down."

"It's only accelerating. I talked with my brother-in-law, and he thinks you should set up a 503c."

"Isn't that like a non-profit?" Ann asks.

"Yep. You could set up a church. It's the best business going."

"I'm never going to be coaching football again, am I?" Ann and Lester tilt their heads. "I need to see my kids."

Ten

The First Supper

Julian gets an early start. The Images of Kathy haunt him. He reminds himself. *The mission is Fred.* Kathy is getting in the way, tweaking his perspective. She is making it hard to stay neutral; he always prided himself on staying neutral. *Damn, she's screwing things up.* He shakes his head. *Enough. Fred. That's the mission.* He scans the list of shooting ranges complied by the FBI, looking up their addresses. First on the list: B and D Indoor Range.

Pulling up to B and D; it looks like a dump. They had taken an old general store, converting it into a gun shop. *Jesus.* The windows are blacked out. Pushing open the door, an electronic buzz announces his arrival. He freezes. A seven-point buck is mounted on the back wall, staring at him with black cold steely eyes. *You don't see one of those much.* The truth is, Julian has never seen one; he's never hunted. He studies the eyes. *Kind of creepy.* He breaks the hypnotic spell the creature has on him.

His eyes skip to the large display cases of pistols lining the left side of the shop. There are six aisles with accessories for purchase. By the cash register is a large open area with three tables and chairs used for classes, and a cute little sign hangs under the register: *I Study Triggernometry.* He chuckles. The steady popping from the shooting range grabs his attention. A stocky man with a tan and green camouflage baseball cap greets him.

"How can I help you?" Kyle asks.

Julian takes in the atmosphere, watching the shooters in range through a large glass window.

"Hi." He flashes his badge. "I'm from Chicago PD."

"Chicago PD? You're a long way from home, aren't ya pal?"

"Yeah, I guess I am."

"You looking to buy a weapon?"

His eyes sweep the pistols cases, resting on Kyle. "Not today. I'm looking for information on one of your patrons."

"Our patrons? Did they do somethin' in Chicago?"

"I'm only collecting some background information. His name is Fred Winters," Julian says.

The man tilts his head with a strange look. "And you say he's one of our patrons?"

"According to the FBI report I've seen, he's one of your patrons."

"Jesus—FBI. Was he in here recently? I'm new here, so—"

Julian smiles, thinking, *I'll just bet you are.* "I'm not sure? I was hoping someone here could tell me."

"That name doesn't ring a bell. Let me get Chet up here. He owns the place."

"Thank you."

The man disappears behind a black curtain. Julian glance at his watch and then looks at the assault rifles mounted on the wall. His eyes sweep down to the pistols in the cases. He peeks at his watch. *What's taking so long?* He turns his attention to the shooters in the range. Chet appears, with Kyle following like a little duckling. Chet is a stocky man with a shooting vest and a pistol strapped to his side.

"Hi, you're with the Chicago PD?" Chet asks.

"Hi, yeah." Julian flashes his badge. "I'm checking on a patron—Fred Winters?"

"I know Fred, whatcha want to know?"

"Does he come in a lot?"

"I don't know. What's a lot? He's been here enough that I know his name."

"I see. What would you say is his skill level—as a shooter?"

"Fred." Chet smiles. "He's a helluva shot."

"What does he usually shoot?"

"What? Like a score?"

"I'm sorry. Weapon, what kind of weapon?"

"I guess mainly nine millimeters."

"Any rifles?"

"What the hell do ya want to know that for?"

"Like I said, it's background."

"We're a small indoor range. It's pistols here." He looks at Kyle, laughing. "We did have this one crazy guy trying to shoot with a rifle." He narrows his eyes. "Did Fred do something?"

"No. When was the last time he was here?"

"Hell, I don't know."

"Okay," Julian smiles. "Thank you for your time."

Julian can overhear Chet talking to Kyle as he exits. "That was crazy. Chicago PD."

With the icy reception he's receiving, Julian stops showing his badge. A theme emerged; Fred is an excellent marksman. Finally, there was a break at the B and D Gun Club. Fred's name is posted as winning a shooting contest, which got Julian thinking, *I wonder if Fred has won any other contests?*

He searches the internet, bringing up twelve shooting ranges. Scratching off the three he'd already visited, there were nine. He scratched off the indoor ranges, which left two. *There, that's manageable. Okay, let's see what I can find.*

Stepping into the Cleveland Armory, he hits pay dirt. On the back wall, Fred's name is posted with numerous awards. Julian approaches the counter.

"How can I help you?"

"Hi, that gentleman posted on the wall back there, Fred Winters." Julian points. The man twists, looking at the board. He twists back to Julian.

He raises an eyebrow. "Yeah, what about him?"

"He's good shooter?"

"As you can see, he wins a lot of contests here."

"Does he coach?"

"Not that I know of."

"I've got a new rifle—it breaks down, you know, like a sniper rifle? I need some instructions on it. Do you think he could help?"

"I'm not sure. What kind of rifle is it?"

"Heck, I'm not sure. It looked so cool, you know, and breaks down into pieces."

"Huh. Well, I'm not sure about Fred. If you like, I can call up Trent. He knows all about the guy."

"He does—that would be great."

Julian waits. A man with a crew cut, broad shoulders, and a pistol strapped to his hip approaches.

"I hear you got some questions about our man on the wall?"

"Yeah, I do. Does he do any coaching?"

"What, you a cop?"

"Nah, I'm a guy who wants to get better at shooting, and it looks like that guy knows what he's doing. How many times has he won your contests?"

"A lot. It's a good thing he doesn't compete every year. Only Sid can give him a run for his money, but Sid has only beaten him once, but I think Fred was sick with a cold that day. Both are ex-military."

"Do ya think he could help with a sniper rifle?"

The man pauses. He wants to say something. Julian gives him a cold stare. "You have a sniper rifle?"

"Yeah, I just bought it."

"Ya know, we have some great coaches here."

"You do. Great, okay, how do I sign up? How much do they charge?"

"It's up to the coach—"

"Have you got a list?"

The man hands him a card. "Here, just go to our website."

Julian scans the card. "Thanks."

"You got it."

Julian says, slipping out the door. The two men shoulder up.

"What do you think? You know, he bought a rifle and didn't know the name."

"I think I smell a cop . . . I think I'll give Fred a call."

"Why do ya think he's asking about sniper rifles?"

"I not sure."

Julian sits in his car, looking at the Cleveland Armory, rubbing his chin. Grabbing his phone, he looks up a special number. He presses the contact number.

"Hey man, it's me. Hey, do you know anyone who's an expert on Marines during the Vietnam war?"

Julian's eyes dart, checking out the restaurant as he follows the host to the table. Waiting for him is a guy named Duke. *Duke. You got to be kidding.* The word from his friend, Duke is ex-CIA analyst, who teaches at some college Julian has never heard of. As luck would have it, the college is in Cleveland. Julian carries a large envelope, which he checks, ensuring that the contents haven't slipped out. He was given one final instruction: don't ask Duke about his background. The host stops, pointing to the table. Duke sits, comfortable, with a bourbon on ice. The two men lock eyes. Duke looks like Trent, back at the Cleveland Armory, crew cut and all, except there's no pistol strapped to his side. *What's with the crew cuts?*

"You Julian?"

Julian nods. "And you're Duke?"

"The one and only." Duke points to the empty chair.

"Thanks for meeting with me."

"You have the right friends. Isn't that the way the world works? Besides, I never miss out on an opportunity for a free dinner—you are buying dinner?"

"Yeah, absolutely."

"Okay then, I'm yours for the evening. What ya drinkin'?"

"Gin and tonic with a twist." The waiter nods and scurries away.

"Chicago PD?"

Julian nods. "Yep."

"You're a bit off the reservation, aren't you?" Duke smiles. Julian nods. "You must be a busy guy?"

Julian raises an eyebrow. "You have no idea—well, maybe you do?"

Duke nods, winking, while he sips. "Whatcha got going on? Vietnam?"

"Yeah."

"That was a long time ago."

"I got a murder I'm working on."

"What makes you think your murder isn't gang-related, or it's not a mob hit?"

"As far as I can tell, the victim wasn't mob-connected, and it's definitely not a gang hit."

"What makes you so sure?"

"It was one bullet. It may be a mob hit, but I have this feeling—"

"One bullet . . . Huh, that's something you don't see much." Julian's drink arrives. "Are you going rogue on this? My understanding is the FBI is looking into this."

"You do your homework."

"I don't just meet with anyone."

"I see. They're running into a wall. I thought I'd do a little freelancing. This thing has got me by the balls."

"Gotcha. You're one of those."

"Uh-huh. It drives my partner crazy."

"You're the kind of guy that would make a good agent," Duke remarks, taking a sip of his bourbon. "Whatcha got?"

"The person of interest is Fred Winters."

"Right. He was in the First Marine Division with Headquarters. He was in admin."

"Wow, you really did do your research?"

"I did," Duke replies.

"Right. Can you look at this picture?" Julian slides a photo out from the envelope, passing it to Duke. "This is a group photo of Fred's unit in Nam."

"Where did you get this?"

"I'd rather not say."

"And judging from the envelope, you have more?"

"I do, but this is the one I was hoping you could help me with."

"Who are we looking—" Duke freezes. He points. "Is this the guy?" Julian twists to see.

"Ahhh . . . Yeah . . . How—"

"The patch."

"The patch?"

"Yep. Look." Duke points to the patch on Fred's arm. "See that skull?" Julian nods. "This guy was a Raider."

"Raider? He was a Marine. What's a Raider?"

"It was a special unit in World War II—actually, it was two units. They only lasted about two years, and they were special ops."

"But this guy was in Nam."

"Right. They were revived, brushed off, so to speak. They upgraded them, and this time it was a very small group. Very specialized. The CIA ran them—very hush-hush—no records. They looked like regular Marines, but they guys were bad assess—black ops."

"Black ops. This guy was black ops." Julian looks closer at the picture. "Shit."

"Look at the others. He's the only one with that patch."

"I see." Julian eyes Duke. "You can tell all that from a patch?"

Duke nods. "Yep." He leans back, sipping his drink. "They had a MOS that made it easy to slip away on special missions. They scattered them in different units like admin, or supply. They would do these special missions like assassinations, kidnappings, things like that. Then, they would return to their units. That was a good way to keep them under wraps."

"Huh." Julian studies the photo and Fred's face. "So, a guy like this—he could—"

"How far was the shot?"

"Roughly 150 feet."

"Shit, he could do a shot like that with his eyes closed. All these Raiders were superior marksman—the best of the best. You know, the kind that could shoot the eye out of an eagle at a hundred yards."

"They scrub their records clean?"

"You got it. If they got caught—"

"They didn't exist."

Duke nods. "Exactly—Even I wouldn't be able to pull anything info up on this guy."

"Wow." Julian tosses the photo and the table, leaning back, sipping his drink.

"What kind of gun was it?"

"We don't know. We found the bullet, but we couldn't run ballistics on it. I'm sure it was a rifle."

"Probably a sniper rifle. What's his connection?"

"The victim shot up his daughter. He actually shot up the whole family, but he really fucked up the daughter. I screwed up and missed him the first time. The FBI was taking a deeper look at him, but he seems to have an alibi."

"I can tell you this—I wouldn't want him after me. These guys were trained to be ghosts, leaving no clues, no loose ends." Duke laughs with hand quotes. "They were 'never there.' Your only clue is one bullet?" Julian nods. "Nothing else?"

"I have footage at the garage where we think he took the shot from. We didn't catch it at first. He altered the plate by putting tape on it."

Duke smiles, taking a sip. "Kind of brilliant."

"Brilliant indeed." Julian grins, picking up the photo, looking again as he takes a sip of his drink. "A Raider."

Julian sits outside Fred's house. *Jesus, a Raider. He was a Raider. I should go in there and say that. See his reaction. Yeah, that's a good plan.* Julian snatches the keys from the ignition and walks up the walkway. Visions of Kathy flood in. He stops. *Damn. Why am I so invested in this? I wanted to know, and now I know.* He glances at his watch. Yeah, it's late. I'll come back tomorrow. He returns to his car.

He works the key card with one hand and a drink he picked up at the Hotel Bar in the other. He shoves the door open and flips the light switch; the door slams shut. "Damn, that was loud." He mutters, places the drink and key card on the table. The room spins. "I think I've had too much to drink." His left arm goes numb. He shakes his arm. "What the fuck?" His heart is racing. "Shit, I need to sit down." He plops his ass on the edge of the bed. The spinning gets worse—he hits the floor hard—convulsing.

Eleven
We May Never Pass This Way Again

Skinny sits in the truck like he's on a stakeout, waiting for nightfall. Lights from a house come on. A streetlamp lights up. Brett's living room light comes on. *I think it's dark enough.* He makes a visual sweep of the neighborhood. *Okay, let's do this thing.* He makes his move. He steps out, careful not to create noise. He presses the truck door until he hears a click. Swiveling his head in both directions, he's monitors for nosy neighbors. *Okay, everything looks cool.*

He darts across the street, holding up at the side of Brett's garage. Leaning against the wall, he watches, listens. *Okay, cool.* He presses onto the gate, popping the latch, pushing the gate open, sneaking inside. With care, he latches the gate. He creeps along the back wall to the garage door. He steals a peek through the window—it's dark. Whipping his head in both directions, he slides a tool out from his back pocket, working the lock. *C'mon man, do your magic.* Click. *Ah, ya still got it, dude.* Pushing the door open, he steps inside. *I should have brought a flashlight.* He stumbles in the dark, taking a few steps to the kitchen door. He gives the knob a twist—it doesn't give. *Damn, it's locked.* He gives it a second try. *I guess you're learning, kid.* He goes to work on the lock. Something inside stirs. He freezes. There's a rumble—footsteps—they're getting louder. *Shit, he's coming.*

Skinny dashes behind the truck, crouching on the driver's side. His breathing is heavy. The door cracks. Brett peers through the slit. Pulling the door open wider, Brett appears with his gun leading the way. He fumbles for the light switch, flicking on the light. His truck sits there, lonely. He cranes his head left and then right. *Was I hearing things?* He listens. *Is that breathing? Am I hearing things?*

"Whoever's in here, I have a gun, and I will shoot your ass." He listens. He waits. Stepping down to the garage floor, he dips his head under the truck, looking, expecting something to jump out. Nothing. *Okay, cool.* The tension in his body relaxes. Relief. He no longer hears breathing. *Am I hearing things? No, something is in here; I can feel it.* He continues his investigation.

Walking toward the garage door, it hits him. *They're in the truck bed.* He pops up, looking. Nothing. Empty. *Huh.* He checks between the garage door and the tailgate. Nothing. *Damn. I must be hearing things.* He moves to the front of the truck. *Nothing here.* He's rounding the driver's side.

Skinny pounces, screaming, "Surprise motherfucker." Brett quivers, which flashes adrenaline through his body, which only serves to freeze him in place. His heart rate spikes, and he's frozen like a mannequin. Skinny latches onto the gun barrel, twisting it toward the wall. Brett fights. They struggle for control. The gun goes off, missing Skinny. Wood chips fly—a stud takes a hit. The struggle is at a stalemate. Skinny grits his teeth, applying more pressure, twisting harder. Brett's wrist gives.

Brett screams, "SHIT."

Skinny throws his elbow, striking Brett's neck. Skinny is quick like a cat, following with a second blow to Brett's head. Brett sees stars. In one fluid motion, Skinny thrusts his hip, flipping him on freezer-chest with a thud. The gun crashes to the floor. Skinny thrusts his forearm into Brett's neck, pinning him. Brett struggles to breathe; he's turning red. Skinny whips out his ice pick, pressing it flat against Brett's cheek—the tip is below his eye. Brett trembles, sweating; he stops kicking.

Skinny whispers like a lover, "Listen here, asshole: you ever pull a gun on me again, I'll blind your ass." Brett can't swallow—he's got no spit. He can't speak. "Blink twice if you understand me." Brett blinks. "Good." Skinny releases him. Brett grabs his neck, massaging it as he nurses himself to a sitting position. He's happy to be breathing. Skinny plunges the ice pick into Brett's left shoulder. The pain shot through Brett's body like an electric shock.

"FUCK."

Withdrawing the ice pick, the blood oozes. Brett clutches his shoulder. Skinny cleans the ice pick by whipping back on forth on Brett's shirt like he's sharpening a knife. Brett doesn't notice; the pain from his shoulder has his focus. He watches the blood seep out, collecting between his fingers.

"Now, where's that motherfucking Billy?"

"What? That's what this is about? I told you I don't know. Fuck. You're a fuckin' psycho."

"That's right bitch, and don't forget it. I figured it out. You two are workin' together—aren't ya?"

"What are you talking about? We're not working together. I barely see the guy—I told ya, I only see 'em at the bar."

"But ya told him about me." Brett's silent "Why'd ya do that?"

"I don't know?"

"He's plotting to kill me, like Pete, ain't he?"

"Why don't you ask him?"

"I would, but I can't find the motherfucker." Skinny fakes another stab with his ice pick. Brett flinches. "Where is the motherfucker?"

"I told you—I don't know. Alright."

"Well, find out. The next time I talk to you, ya better know." Skinny collects the gun, raising it up, considering its weight. He looks through the sights. "Nice." They lock eyes. "Thanks. Next time—ya fuckin' better know." Skinny slips out the way he came.

Brett rocks. His arm quivers. *That motherfucker. Fuck. God, I hate that motherfucker!* He tends to his shoulder. Blood covers his shoulder and fingers. "Fuck."

Skinny tosses the gun into the glove box. *Now, don't forget it's in there.* He sighs. Looking perplexed, he starts the truck. He stares, contemplating. *Now what?* Putting the truck into gear, he's not sure where he's going. He trolls the streets. Like magic, he is on Hiler Avenue; Sterling City is a small town. Killing the headlights, he creeps in front of Sylvia's house. The brakes squeak as he brings the truck to a stop. The house is dark. His eyes dart to the house across the street—it's also dark. He chuckles. *Fun neighborhood.* He glances at the time—it's 7:30. *That's not that late. Where does that dirt road on the side go? Billy came flying out of there.* Releasing the brakes, he lets the truck roll to the mouth of the road. He stops. *Huh, it looks like it goes to the back of the house. I'm intrigued, let's see where this little road goes.*

The tires crunch the gravel. The road runs alongside the fence to the yard, curling to a large opening. *Look at this. I'm going to guess this is where Billy parks his truck.* The only light that shines is from the back porch. An old chicken coop is straight ahead. A barn is off to the left. He cranes his head, looking at a streetlight mounted on the peak of the barn—it's dark. *Is it burned out or just not on?* The pathway leading to the back pouch grabs his attention. The area is lined with large trees, making it secluded. He kills the engine—observing. Nothing is stirring. No dogs are barking. *Where is everyone?*

He slips out of the truck. With a measured gait, he works his way up the path—his head is on a swivel, monitoring for anything that might jump out. Making it to the backdoor, he gives a final glance over his shoulder before twisting the knob—it gives—it's open. *What the? Is this a trap? The last time a door was open, I got my ass shot.* He's not eager to enter. Spending a little more time sizing up the situation, he peers through a window. *Looks empty.* He peeks over his shoulder. He's alone. Focusing back on the door, he gives it a light push—it doesn't give. *Fuck, what is it—a deadbolt?* He inspects. "Fuck." He gives the knob a violent shake. A loud grinding noise cries out. Skinny laughs. *It sticks, fucking-A.* With a light step, he enters. Moonbeams stream through the large window, giving enough light to see. He looks for a light switch, but he decides to move in the dark; there's enough light so that he's not bumping into anything. *Damn, I should have brought the gun. I guess my ice pick will have to do.* The further he creeps into the house, the darker it gets.

Making it to the living room, one thing is certain, Sylvia's place is a mess. Lipstick-stained glasses, used plates, and coffee mugs decorate the coffee table. On the end table, there's an open grease-stained pizza box with an old, dried-up slice of pizza. *Yum.* A stack of opened and unopened mail sits atop the table against the wall. *Man, this woman is a slob. I wonder where she is? Shit, I think I know.* He returns the way he came.

Back in the truck, he gives one final survey. *This place is kinda creepy.*

Skinny enters the Cue Ball. It's busy. Two people tend bar. One is a female. *Could it be? It sure looks like her.* Skinny didn't get a good look at Sylvia standing on her porch. *Wow, this place is hopping. Where do all these people come from?* He approaches the bar, which is three deep. Fighting the crowd, he weasels his way to the bar. Sylvia and Tim fly back and forth, filling orders—it's non-stop action. Skinny doesn't exist; no nod, no *I'll be with you soon.* It gives Skinny a chance to study Sylvia.

Skinny's thoughts run wild. *She moves with grace. She's focused. She's confident. How is it this woman is such a slob?* He's so lost in thought he doesn't notice Tim staring at him.

"Liking the scenery?" Tim asks.

"Sorry . . . Ah, yeah."

"Did you get in a fight?"

Skinny touches his knot. He chuckles. "Yeah, with a steering wheel."

"Oh. What can I get ya? Wait a second, you're that guy—" Skinny nods. "Are you stalking her?"

"No, man, it's not what you think."

"What am I thinking?"

"Ah . . . Nothing. Give me a whiskey, neat," Skinny says. Tim stares at him. *I think this dude is going to hit me.* "Is there a problem?"

"Nah," Tim replies. Moving to the shelves, he grabs a bottle of Jack. He leans toward Sylvia, whispering. Sylvia nods and then glances at Skinny before heading to the restroom. Skinny tries to follow, but he's trapped against the bar. He fights, working his way out. Free, he's got a good sight line on Sylvia's movements. Sylvia ducks into the women's room. Like a shark, his got his prey in sight. Thump—A bat is planted in his chest. His eyes travel up the bat to who holds it—Tim. Tim has a devious grin. *What the fuck?*

"What's up, dude?" Tim asks. This attracts the attention from a few guys within ear shot. This is about to get ugly. Skinny throws his arms in the air like it's a stickup.

Skinny smiles. "It's all good, man." His bad shoulder is screaming—he keeps smiling. "It's all good."

"That's good to hear. I think it's time ya left."

A guy close by nods. "Yeah, motherfucker."

"Who is this asshole?" another asks.

Tim smiles; it's the kind of smile that says, *please give me an excuse.* Skinny shuffles backward. His eyes bounce between Tim and the three guys itching to pounce. *Okay, man, don't push a bad position. Just ease out of this place.*

"Okay, okay, man. It's all cool." He backs out the front door. The door swings closed. *Damn, that was fucked up.* He stares at the door. He glances at the neon signs in the window. *Fuck. Damn. Now what?* He returns to the truck.

He stews, watching, studying, plotting his next move. *Okay, time to regroup.* Sylvia pops out of the back of The Cue Ball, walking fast. *Well, lookie here.* Sylvia's pace is brisk as she hurries down Main Street. Skinny fires up the truck. *Looks like it's my lucky day, or night.* He chuckles. Throwing the truck into gear, he's ready to pounce. A truck races by, cutting him off. They miss each other by inches. Skinny's heart skips a beat. *Shit, that was close.* The driver stops in front of Sylvia. After a short conversation, she hops in. *Who the hell is that? Is that Billy?* It's too dark to tell for sure. *I'll bet it's him.* The truck is off, moving fast down Main Street. *Boy, if that is Billy, my night just got luckier.* Skinny pulls out to follow.

The truck blows through the stop sign at Main and 1st Street; this is where Main becomes Hiler. *Crap, they're trying to get away.* Skinny punches the gas pedal, trying to close the gap. He blows through the stop sign. He breaks at the curve of Hiler as he comes upon Sylvia's place. He brings the truck to a crawl, observing the house. The house is dark.

Maybe they're not inside yet? Or are they hiding in that barn outback? Or are they hiding in the house? Hell, maybe they're in there, watching me right now? He kills the headlights. He glances at the time on the dash. *I wish I had a gun. Oh, shit, I do.* He flips open the glove box, retrieving the gun. *Is this thing even loaded?* He releases the magazine. He didn't have to look—it's heavy. *Shit, that's right, it went off at Brett's place what the fuck am I thinking.* He jams the magazine back in, cocking it. The house remains dark. *Yeah, I'll bet those assholes are hiding back in that barn.*

Leaving the headlights off, he puts the truck in gear. He's a hunting machine, gliding, waiting to strike. Stopping at the mouth of the dirt road, the road is clear—he drives forward. Clearing a giant oak tree, the barn comes into view. He settles in the clearing, glancing at the old chicken coop, and then to the house. His eyes dart from the chicken coop to the barn to the house. There's no truck. There's no car. *Isn't this fucked up. Where are ya, motherfuckers?* He studies the barn. *Did they drive in there? Yeah, yeah, that's what I would do.* He kills the engine. His eyes lock on the house—it's still dark. *Yeah, they're not in the house.* He focuses back on the barn. *I'll bet you two are in there, aren't ya?*

Slipping out of the cab, the gun at the ready. His footsteps are soft like a dancer's. His head swivels, monitoring as he sneaks toward the barn, looking like he's out of a spy movie. He sizes up the doors—they're huge. He pries open the left door; the hinges creak. He slips inside. He can't see shit. He didn't have to. The barn is empty. *Damn, they slipped me. Fuck.* The barn smells musty, transporting him back to when he was a kid playing in the neighbor's barn. An engine outside breaks his daydream. *An engine? Shit—someone is coming.* He presses his back to the door, pushing to create a crack to get a view of another truck that has parked behind his. *Great, the motherfucker blocked me in.* The lights are off. The motor is running. His truck blocks the sight line; he can't see who's in the other truck. *How many of them are there? Are they the guys from the bar? Did they follow me? I'll bet that's it, they followed me.* He sweats. As the beads of sweat form on his brow, one drips into his eye, blurring his vision. He wipes his eye and brow with his sleeve. *So how many of them are there? Maybe it's Billy and that bitch? They doubled back on my ass.* No footsteps. No voices. No doors shutting—the truck engine hums. *Why don't they show themselves? They're trying to mind-fuck me. Jesus, this is fucked up. No, it's probably those guys from the bar.*

He sees something—darting. *What was that? Damn, it was so fast. It could be anything. Okay, calm down. Think. Think this out. Jesus, how many of them are there? The best move is to wait.* He eases the barn door closed. *Yeah, wait. Do they have weapons? What the fuck, of course they have weapons, and if I run out of here, they'll mow my ass down. That's it, isn't it? They want me to run out there so they can mow me down.* The sweat builds on his hand—the gun is slipping. He switches the pistol to the other hand, wiping the sweat on his pants. *It's been too long. What are they doing? Waiting here by the door is no good. All they have to do is open this door, and it's a turkey shoot, and I'm the fucking turkey. I need to change my vantage point. I can't see shit. But, if I can't see shit, they can't either. Hold it, I'll wait here, they'll get antsy, run in here, and I can mow their asses down. Yeah, that's good.* He stumbles around, finding a stall. He crouches behind a small wood slat and post, gun at the ready. *Yeah, this is better.*

He hears a second engine coming closer. *Great, more of them. I'll bet it's those fuckin' guys from the bar.* Doors slam. Two male voices are in a discussion. *What are they planning?* He shakes. *Why am I shaking? Maybe I've been crouching too long.* His muscles burn. He falls back on his ass, landing in a pile of hay. *Oh God, that's better.* He sets the gun aside, rubbing his legs. He basks in relief. A chain rattles. *What? A chain? Fuck, they're goin' to lynch me. Drag my ass behind a truck? Well, fuck that noise—I'm not goin' to get dragged behind a truck.* He reaches for the pistol—it's gone—the hay ate it. *What? No, no, no.* He flips to his knees. *Oh man, where the fuck are you?* His digs, searching. Kicking up dust. *Oh, c'mon, where are you?* The dust is thick—he needs to sneeze. He plugs his nose, sneezing. His ears pop—he farts. He freezes. *Did they hear that?* He listens. The truck engine is loud. *Okay, probably not.*

He continues his search. His hand brushes against the gun. *Found it. Yes.* He grabs it, yanking it up; he has a poor grip on it—it flies—somewhere. He's not sure which direction. He's back to hunting. *Dammit, where are you?* The commotion outside grabs his attention. *Air brakes?* A diesel engine rev. *What's going on now? That's a big rig.* He stops searching for the gun and slinks to the doors. He snuggles against the door, waiting, listening. *Man, that's a big truck.* He leans on the door, creating a crack. He peeks.

His truck is moving. *What the hell!* A tow truck is dragging his truck away. He vaults open the door, rushing out to give chase. Crack. His head rings like a bell. His vision goes sideways—he can't focus. His knee hits first, kicking up a plume of dust. His face slaps the dirt, kicking up a bigger plume of dust. His body twitches.

Brett dances, announcing, "And the crowd goes wild." Brett stands over Skinny with a bat resting on his shoulder. "You're not looking so good, man." Skinny is still. He wipes the bat on Skinny's shirt. "Ya gotta keep your tools clean, right cousin." He bends over for a closer look, placing two fingers on Skinny's neck—no pulse. "Yes." Brett jumps up, mocking a home run swing. "Good riddance, cousin. Say good-bye to your pincushion." He tosses the bat on his good shoulder and limps to his truck. *I wonder how Tim knew? Thanks for the address, Tim.* Checking the wound on his shoulder, blood oozes from the dressing. "Okay, now it's time to get stitched up."

Tom stands at the sliding glass door, waiting. Fred pushes back the curtain. They lock eyes—no emotion is exchanged. Fred slides open the door.

"Ya alone?" Fred asks.

"Yeah. It took a bit before I could lose them." Tom stomps his feet, shaking the snow off his shoes.

"Those media people?"

"Man, it's cold out there. No, they don't bother me anymore—ever since Oprah. The groupies still hound me."

The kids bust in. "Daddy, Daddy."

Tom scoops them up. "Oh, I've missed you guys."

"Daddy, Mommy is back," Amber remarks

"I heard."

"She's in the front room," Peetie says.

"Let's go see her." Tom carries them into the front room.

Kathy sits with a vacant stare; the TV is on but she's not watching. It serves as background noise. Tom stops, letting the kids down.

Fred whispers, "It's all she's done since she got home."

Tom nods. "Kathy?"

Amber runs to Kathy. "Mommy, Mommy, Daddy is here." Kathy breaks her stare, looking at Amber.

"What?"

"Daddy is here."

Tom moves further into the room. Kathy gives Tom a slight glance.

"Oh, look, the rock star is here."

"Hi, Kathy. How are you?"

She shrugs. "I've been better. Hey, Dad, can you take the kids?"

"Sure." Fred corrals the kids, sweeping them into the next room.

Tom is anxious; he's wondered about this moment, not sure what to expect. He knew he was going to get an ear full—Kathy style. He waits, anticipating, expecting a raw emotional outburst. It doesn't come. She is docile as an old hound dog on a hot summer's day—almost lifeless, except, she moves, well kind of. Whatever life is breathing within those bones, has been neutered.

There are these moments in life where you think you're prepared, but when confronted the reality, it's nothing like what you had built up in your mind. This is one big punch to the gut—he's shaken. Tom gazes upon his broken wife; something within shattered—his mouth drops. *Where's that cocky, salty woman? She's in there, isn't she?* He studies her face, waiting for something, anything, a spark maybe to let him know it's Kathy, well, the Kathy he knows. She stares off. That woman is gone; she's a shell of her old self. *Oh God, she's broken.* He chokes up. His eyes well up.

He flashes on the brick from that night back in Big Springs. His life has been in such chaos since then. He's been grappling to put order or some sense to it; all that melts away as meaningless. Up to now, he's been the victim, or so he thought. He's staring at the biggest casualty. *What have I done? I pushed. I force us to Big Springs. She fought so hard not to go. Now look at her.* He struggles to compose himself—to say something. He clears his throat.

"I hear you're getting better." *Shit, that was lame. Dammit man, you can do better than that.*

She shrugs. "I guess. I still can't use my arm. I can finally breathe normally again. Thank God I can walk, so I guess that's something."

Their eyes lock. Tom breaks—a tear dribbles down his cheek—he's quick to trap it, wiping it away. "Why are you crying? You're out there running around having a grand time. I'm the one stuck in this chair."

His voice shakes, "I'm not having a grand time."

"It sure looks like it from where I'm sitting. What's wrong with you? You got what you wanted. You always get what you want."

"Kathy, I'm so sorry," Tom says.

"I know." She stares at the TV. It's awkward. They sit in silence. It's icy. Tom fidgets.

Is she going to say something? Oh my God, what have I done. After all that time spent waiting in hospitals, this is so much worse than he imagined. He flooded with visions of her shot, bleeding back at the Auto Body Shop.

She looks at him. "You know, I've had a lot of time to think." Tom nods. "And I think it's time to part ways."

Tom nods, clearing his throat. "That's probably best."

"Are we going to have any issues with the kids?"

"I still want them in my life."

"Of course. I want that too. But will you ever be able to see them? I mean, what are you doing? Are you going back to that hell hole? Moving on with your nurse? Traveling all over God knows where?"

"Big Springs is over. I'm not sure about the rest."

It's like the TV is a magnet, sucking her eyes; she's back staring at the screen. Silence. "I thought they wanted you back?"

Tom is unnerved, having a conversation with someone who's not looking at you.

"They do. But things have changed."

"Huh."

Tom squirms. More silence. Tom can't take it anymore—he stands, clearing his throat.

"Anything you want. I'll agree to it," Tom says. Kathy gazes at him, lost. "I'll agree to anything you want."

"Oh, okay." She returns her gaze to the TV. "Whatever."

He wants to leave—he's frozen. It's like he is abandoning someone in a burning car, but this isn't just someone; it's his wife, the mother of his children. *God, this sucks.* Tom gets his leg to move and wanders into the kitchen. Now he's the one with the vacate look.

Fred sits at the breakfast bar, drinking coffee. They lock eyes, sharing the pain.

"Sad, isn't it." Fred remarks.

Tom nods. They turn, watching the kids play in the family room. Tom breaks the silence.

"About that part?" Tom asks.

"Part?"

"You know."

"Oh, that."

"Was it worth it?"

"You don't get me, do you? I'd do anything for my daughter, anything. That goes for my grand kids. You, well."

"Yeah." Tom nods. "How are the kids?"

"Whatcha asking? There's not much laughing going on around here if that's what ya want to know."

"Yeah. Damn," Tom remarks.

They're in the same space, talking, but they're in their own worlds, numb. Fred breaks the silence.

"You know, I thought she'd bounce back, but now I'm not so sure."

Tom nods.

Billy and Sylvia are locked in a conversation about Skinny. He turns onto the road on the side of her house. He stops.

"What going on?" she asks.

He whips his head; they lock eyes. "I'll bet he's waiting for us."

"Oh God, that's an awful thought." She glances at her house. "I just got chills. Why don't we stay at your place tonight?"

Billy stares, considering her request. "No, I'm sick of this shit. I just want it over."

"It's not going to be great if *it's over* means we're both dead. Can't we stay at your place tonight?"

"We could—Yeah, maybe you're right. Let me get turned around." Billy drives into the clearing. "I don't see that piss-yellow Caddy."

"Knowing he's out there gives me the creeps. Can we go?" Sylvia asks.

"Why go if he's not here? He's shown up at my place. What's the difference?

"I don't know? You know he's going—"

"What's that?"

"What?"

"There." Billy points. "By the barn. Is that a body?" Billy maneuvers the truck, shining the headlights on the lump. "Shit, it's a body."

"Billy, I don't like this. Let's go to your place and call the Sheriff."

"What if they need help?"

"Billy, I don't like this. You don't know who that is and what the hell are they doing back here?"

"Are they moving? I don't think they're moving. Maybe I should check?"

"No, call 911. C'mon, let's go. This is creepy. This is a trick."

"Yeah, maybe . . . I don't know? Hand me my pistol—It's in the glove box."

"C'mon, Billy, let's go."

"It will be alright." Billy bends across Sylvia, opening the glove box. Snatching the pistol, he cocks it, making sure it's loaded. Reaching under his seat, he grabs a flashlight. He steps out—cautious—taking measured steps toward the body. He flashes the light toward the house, then the chicken coop, and then the body. "Hey, do you need help?"

Are they breathing? He sweeps the light toward the chicken coop and then the house before resting the light back on the body. The gun shakes. *Shit, dude, calm down.* He presses on. "Hey, are you okay?"

He stands over the body, studying, looking for any movement. The body is still. *I guess it would be hard to breathe with your face buried in the dirt like that.* He gives a slight kick to the arm. *Jesus, his neck is crooked.* He steps over the head. *Shit, the back of his head is bashed in.* Blood is dribbling from the base of the head, pooling in the dirt. *Man, it doesn't look like he's been here long.* He throws the light on the barn, and then back to the body. *Whoever did this, are they still here?* He casts the light on the barn doors.

Sylvia yells, "Okay, ya checked. C'mon. Let's go."

"Just a second." Billy moves to the barn doors, pulling open a door, sliding inside. Sylvia honks the horn. He pops out of the barn, directing his light on Skinny.

He cocks his head. "I think they're dead?"

"Good. Can we go now?"

"I think it's that Skinny guy."

"Okay, good. Let's go."

Billy bends to roll the body over.

Sylvia screams, "Don't touch anything."

Billy freezes. "Yeah, I guess you're right." Billy returns to the truck. She waits for him to start driving.

She's not happy. "What are you doing? Let's go." Billy stares at the chicken coop. "Billy, what's going on?"

He looks at her. "Ya know, if that's Skinny—"

"Yeah. What about Skinny? He's a creep."

"I know. Ya know he's Brett's cousin?"

"Right. So?"

"Ya know that guy I ran over in Chicago?"

"Yeah?"

"Well . . . Um . . . Ah—"

"Billy, what's going on?"

"Crap, they were best friends."

"What are you talking about? How do you know that?"

"Brett told me."

"Okay . . . So, what?"

"It's . . . It's just—it's going to be very strange if I'm around both guys deaths, don't ya think?"

"Okay, what's going on? What aren't you telling me?"

Billy sighs. "I don't know. Fuck—This really sucks. That cop in Chicago, he put me in that room, grilling me. He was busting my balls."

"Yeah, but you're here. So what? What are you saying?"

"Oh, I don't know. How about we like, move the body? You know, like somewhere else?"

"WHAT! No way. We are not touching anything! You can forget that noise. You can take off, or whatever, but we're not—"

"Okay, okay. You're right. Let's call the Sheriff.

Twelve

Put Out an APB

Ann stares at the keypad, trying to remember the code. Rummaging through her purse, she pulls out a posted note with five numbers. Her fingers dance across the keypad. The beeping stops and the red-light switches to green. She notes the time. Flipping on the lights, she's feeling better—dark buildings have always felt creepy to her. She shivers—it's chilly. Fiddling with the thermostat, the heater switches on.

Walking through the halls, her footsteps echo. Pushing the door open to the green screen room, she notices the computer on with the screen saver active. A camera sits mounted on a tripod, pointed at the green sheet. This is where all the magic happens.

Settling into the chair at the desk, she watches the screen saver draw patterns. She glances at her watch. *Where is everyone? I can't believe I beat them here? Where's Lester? Damn, it's cold. I didn't know I needed a coat.* It's lonely. She fidgets. *Where are they? Enough of this noise.*

She calls Tom. The call goes to voicemail. *Tom, where are you? And why haven't you called me? Let me know what's going on. I love you.* She tosses the phone on the desk. *Isn't this fun?*

Twenty minutes pass. She picks up the phone.

"Oh hi, I'm checking in to see when Tom got on the plane?"

"I'm sorry we haven't called. He still hasn't called to have the car pick him up. You never said how long he was staying?"

"Huh. Okay, thank you." *Tom, where are you?* Another call to Tom. It goes to voicemail. *Jesus, where are you?* She doesn't leave a message. *Maybe Lester has heard from—what am I thinking, why wouldn't he be calling me?* She caresses her face, contemplating. She pops the phone to her ear.

"Hi, girlfriend," Kay answers.

"Hi."

"What's wrong?"

"How do you do that?"

"Do what?"

"Know when something is wrong?"

"It's not hard. It's the tone in your voice."

"Huh, you're damn good at it."

"Somethings happen."

"He's gone," Ann says.

"Tom?"

"Yeah. And I'm sitting in this big ass studio—alone, waiting for him."

"What studio?"

"It's the VR thing—for Tom."

"VR?"

"Yeah, sorry. It's a long story. We were supposed to meet about two hours ago. The last time I talked with him was early yesterday." Lester enters. Ann waves.

"Is this like last time?"

"No, this is different. Let me call you back."

"Okay."

"Hi, Ann. Where's Tom?" Lester asks.

"Hi. He hasn't shown up."

Lester glances at his watch. "What? I thought we were meeting. Sorry I'm late. It is today, right?"

"Yes."

"Has he called?"

"No. I've called him, but my calls are going to voicemail."

"Huh."

"He never called to have the driver pick him up."

"He's still in Cleveland? Is he still at his father-in-law's?"

"Maybe? I don't know. He's not answering my calls."

"Has he done this before?"

"No. You try him," Ann says.

"You think he's ghosting you? Really? You?" Ann shrugs. "What if something happened to him?"

"That's possible. Try him."

"Okay," Lester calls. He listens to the message. "Hi, Tom, Lester here. Give me a call when you get this." Lester looks at his phone, and then at Ann.

"You handle the money. Has there been any big withdrawals lately?"

"Wait a second. You think he's running away?"

"I don't know what to think," Ann remarks.

"I'm not sure. We've been moving money into a checking account lately—you know, for expenses. But I have limited access to that account, for, you know, I can only put money in." He logs onto the computer. "Wait a second, I can look at the account we set up offshore."

"You can?"

"Sure." He punches the keyboard. "Huh."

"Do you see something?"

"Nope. Nothing has gone out."

"That figures."

"He's not at his father-in-law's?" Lester asks.

"Maybe, but why isn't he returning my calls?" Ann asks.

Lester shrugs. "When did he go there?"

"Yesterday."

"Which means what? He spent the night?"

"Right."

"Let me check to see if there's been a sighting. His disciples are good at tracking him."

"Disciples? Is that what they're called these days?"

"Yep." Lester is back working the keyboard. "Crap."

"What, what?"

"He seems to have slipped them. There's some chatter about trying to figure out where he is, but they don't seem to know where he is either. The last sighting was in Cleveland."

"Damn. He's gone back to her," Ann mutters.

"Her? His wife? What?"

"Oh, nothing . . . I should call Kay." She throws the phone to her ear.

"That was fast," Kay remarks.

"Lester showed up. We were putting our brains together."

"What did you come up with?"

"Nothing. Except maybe he spent the night at his father-in-law's."

"Call him."

"Fred?"

"Yeah."

"I can't do that."

"Go there."

"I can't do that either. Kathy is there."

"She's out of the hospital?"

"Yeah."

"Oh shit," Kay remarks.

"What?"

"I know what you're thinking."

"It has crossed my mind."

"Now, Ann, don't get going. You don't know what's going on yet. Maybe something happened. Don't be jumping to conclusions, girlfriend."

"Like what? He lost his phone?"

"Maybe?"

"Yeah, well—"

"Ann—"

"I know. I know you're right. But it's hard," Ann remarks.

"I can't call Fred—maybe you could call Cindy. What about Cindy?"

"I don't know Cindy. *You* know Cindy."

"Okay. Let me see what I can find out."

"Oh, thank you so much." She drops the phone, staring off.

"Maybe he needed some space?" Lester offers. "Or—"

"What, or what?"

"Do you think he's been abducted?"

The Sheriff's SUV pulls alongside Billy's truck; Deputy Jerry Green emerges. Billy, leaning against his truck, stands. Sylvia climbs out of the truck.

"Is that you, Billy?"

"Hi, Jerry."

"How do, Ms. Sylvia?"

"Hey, Jerry."

"What ya guys into? Mark said something about a body?" Billy points to the lump. "Holy shit." Jerry pulls his flashlight like a warrior drawing a light saber. "Who is that?"

"I don't know, but I got my suspicions," Billy remarks.

"Ya do?"

"Yeah, but I'm guessing."

"Did ya touch anything?"

"No, that's how we found him," Billy says.

Jerry throws his light at the barn, then the chicken coop, over to the backyard, and back to Skinny. Approaching the body, he sweeps the light on the ground. Bending over the body.

He looks back at the couple with a nervous laugh. "I've never seen a dead body." They smile. "Kinda hard to breathe with your face planted in the dirt like that, isn't it?"

"Ya know, I was thinking the same thing," Billy remarks.

Jerry nods. Placing two fingers on the neck, he checks for a pulse. Nothing. He throws the light on the base of Skinny's head. "Look at that. Looks like he was whacked in the head . . . Baseball bat, or tire iron, maybe?" He studies. "Nah, I'm goin' ta guess it was a bat." He stands, wiping his hands on his pants as he faces the couple. "Ya say you know who this is?"

"I'm guessing it's Skinny," Billy replies.

"Skinny who?"

"Brett's cousin."

"Brett's gotta cousin?"

"Yep."

"Tell me again. What happened?"

"We drove in and saw the body. I got out and checked him out—you know, with my flashlight. I checked the barn, in case whoever did this was still here, and then we called you."

"I see." Jerry sweeps the light over the area, calculating how Skinny ended at his final resting spot. "I'm guessing he came out of this barn, and someone whacked him." He ponders. He walks, examining the ground close to the barn door. "Yeah, look at this. The ground is all tamped down over here. They probably waited here." He looks at them. "I guess I should call the Sheriff."

Within thirty minutes, the place is crawling with law enforcement. The barn doors are open and County forensics are combing through the barn. The place is lit up with portable lights. Sheriff Martin Clark stands over Skinny.

"You two know who this unfortunate soul is?" Martin asks.

"No, sir," Sylvia replies.

"Billy."

"I got my hunch."

"Okay." Martin slides out a wallet from Skinny's back pocket. "Let's see if this will enlighten us." He fingers through the cards; he comes upon the driver's license. "Okay let's see, who we got? Looks like it's Theodore Fredrick Hart. Is this guy kin to Brett?"

"I've never heard that name before, Sheriff," Billy says.

"Me neither."

"He's not from around here. It looks like he's from Big Springs."

Billy's mind goes into overdrive, drawing a flowchart; Skinny to Pete—Chicago—back to him. Brett to Skinny—Skinny to Pete—Chicago—back to him. Skinny is dead at Sylvia's—all roads lead to Billy. *Damn, I knew we should have gotten rid of the body.*

"If this guy is from Big Springs, and neither one of you whacked him, who knew he was here? And, more importantly, why was he here? What's in his other pocket?" Martin tugs on the ice pick. "An ice pick?" Martin holds it up. "Who carries an ice pick? Hey Jerry, can you bag this?" Martin rolls Skinny face up. "So what? Is this guy homeless?"

"Oh shit," Sylvia mumbles.

"Ya know him?"

"Ya, I think that's that Skinny dude?"

"He goes by Skinny?"

"Ya, I guess so. That's what I hear. He was at The Cue Ball earlier tonight. Tim chased him out of the place."

"Tim. So what time was that?"

"I don't know for sure, but maybe around 7:30."

Martin checks his watch. "Why did Tim chase him out of The Cue Ball?"

"He told me that he thought he was stalking me."

"I see. So, a man that may have been stalking you gets kicked out of The Cue Ball, and what, stumbles down Main Street to here? Did he know where you lived?" Martin asks.

"I'm not sure," Sylvia says.

Martin looks at Jerry. "Were there any vehicles found?"

"No Sheriff. Just the body."

"Okay, no vehicle," Martin remarks. "Now what is that on his forehead? Looks like he got hit in the front, too? Christ, he's been hit in the front, and then the final blow to the back. A tag team maybe?"

"Wow," Billy cringes. *Damn, I'm going to get sucked into this thing—I can feel it. We should have moved the body.*

"You say Tim chased him out of The Cue Ball?"

"Yes, Sheriff," Sylvia replies.

"Do you know if things got rough?"

"I'm not sure."

"Man, this all stinks." Martin studies the knot on Skinny's forehead. "Seems kinda odd that a man from Big Springs would be afoot?"

"Maybe he parked up the street and walked in," Jerry offers.

There's a yell from inside the barn. "We got something."

Martin and Jerry rush in.

"Whatcha got?" Martin asks.

"A gun."

They gaze at the gun partially buried in the hay.

Martin yells, "Sylvia, can you come in here?"

She rushes in. "Yes, Sheriff?" Billy is in tow.

"Is this your gun?"

She looks. "It's not mine. I only have a shotgun."

Martin eyes Billy. "Billy, is this yours?"

Billy's face contorts. "Hell no, mine's in my truck." *Jesus, now there's a gun. We should have moved the body.*

"If this isn't the damnedest thing?" Martin remarks, sliding a pen in the barrel, hoisting it up. "A mystery man found with a mystery gun and the man is whacked a few feet away. Is that something." He rubs his chin. "Sylvia, how often do you go in this barn?"

"It's been a while. There's nothing much I need in here. I got rid of all the livestock when my daddy died—I don't even have chickens, anymore."

He nods. "I see." Martin eyes the gun. "Look at that, the guns not rusted. It looks like it's been well taken care of. So, it hasn't been here that long." He rubs his chin. "It looks like someone recently rolled around in this stall, doesn't it?" He looks at the forensics agent.

"I believe that is correct," he replies.

"Ya think it was a fight?"

"I'm going to say no. The hay isn't mashed down. It's almost like it's been fluffed up—someone was maybe hunting for it?"

"Right." Martin stands. "Let's say he was in here, hiding out, and for some reason was drawn out, and got whacked?" Martin rubs his chin. "Why wouldn't he bring the gun? If it was his gun? Hell, none of this makes any Goddamn sense." Martin locks eyes with Billy. "Unless, Billy, you sure you don't have something to tell me?"

Here we go. "I've been with Sylvia since she left The Cue Ball tonight."

"It's true, Sheriff. He picked me up, and we've been driving around until we came back here and found him face down in the dirt."

Martin studies Billy's eyes. "Okay, bag the gun."

Perez scans his computer monitors. An officer stops.

"Hey, Perez, the captain wants to see you."

Perez tilts his head, eyeing the captain's office. He nods. *What the hell does he want?* He pushes back from his desk and makes the journey to his office. He stands at the door; it's open. The captain is on the phone. Perez knocks, waiting for the go ahead to enter. The captain's head snaps, locking eyes with Perez. He waves Perez in. He points to the chair in front of his desk. He ends his call. He sighs, leaning back.

"How are you doing?"

Perez shrugs. "Okay."

"I got some bad news. I wanted you to know, you know, before the rumor mill gets going out there."

Perez perks up. "Okay."

"Julian died."

"What?" The captain nods. "How?"

The captain scratches his head. "He was found in a hotel room. He had a heart attack."

Perez tilts his head. "Hotel room? What hotel room? Where?"

"Cleveland."

"Jesus, that guy. So, that's where he went?"

"I guess. He took a leave of absence, but he didn't tell me anything. So, he didn't tell you?"

"Nah." Perez stares off. "Fuckin' Cleveland." He combs his fingers through his hair. "Well, damn."

"Anyway, I wanted to hear it first. Why don't you take the rest of the day off. If you need more time, give me a call."

Perez nods. "I'll bet he was freelancing on that hostel case."

"I'm going to guess you're right. He requested the time right after the powwow with the FBI."

"So, what the hell was said?"

"He didn't tell you?"

"He doesn't tell me shit. He was the worst and best partner I've ever had."

"I always said he was like herding a cat."

"So, what was he chasing?"

"I don't know. He got this weird look when the father-in-law of that coach once he found out he was in the Marines."

"Who?"

The captain picks a file out from his desk and flips open the folder. He rifles through the papers, plucking a sheet out. "Fred Winters."

"I don't remember that name."

"Well, he did. He latched on it like a dog with a bone."

Sam pulls his Sheriff's vehicle to a stop. He sighs, staring at the mobile home. A curtain moves. He knows she is watching. He slides out of his car, sliding his nightstick into his holster. Tracy opens the door. They share a look.

"Ahh, shit," she says. Sam progresses toward the door.

"I'm real sorry, Tracy."

Her eyes well up. "Damn, damn, damn. Where did they find him?"

"Sterling City."

"What?" She gets angry. "That fucking guy. His car was in the shop there."

"It was?"

"Ya, he fucked it up. It's probably ready to be picked up."

"Okay, Tracy what's goin' on. Why has he messin' around in Sterling City?" She shrugs. "The Sheriff down there was wondering."

"Wondering what?"

"Where his vehicle was?"

"His Caddy was in the shop. He had me borrow Old Man Jenkin's truck. That's what he's been driving."

"The Sheriff over there said there was no Caddy or Truck."

"Where'd they find him?"

"In front of a barn."

"What barn?"

"It was a small property down there. He'd been hit in the forehead and then hit in the back of the head with something—they haven't figured that part out yet. But he got in a tussle with someone."

"The forehead was when he fucked up his car. He smacked his head on the steering wheel. He wouldn't talk too much about it. He looked like a frickin' freak like he was growin' a horn." She chuckles. "Just like a fuckin' unicorn. Lately, he's been real secretive about what he's been doing."

"I'll pass that along."

"Jesus. I knew this was going to happen someday." She returns to sadness.

"What was Skinny into these days? Word has it he took a ride to Chicago?"

"Shit, I don't know? Like I said—the only thing he would say is the less I knew the better." A tear leaks from her eye.

"He's dead. Ya don't have to protect him anymore."

"Shit . . . He's dead." She stares at the ground. The tears flow.

It's awkward as she cries. Her face contorts as she wipes her eyes, blowing her nose. She wants to say something, but she can't.

"C'mon, Tracy. A good confession would be good for the soul."

Tracy nods, the tears flow. "Shit, I don't know, he was focused on this Billy guy. I don't know anything more than that. He wanted him real bad."

"Billy?" Sam tilts his head. "This guy keeps poppin' up. Is that the one that ran over Pete?"

She shrugs. The tears stopped. "I don't know, maybe?"

"Tracy, I'm real sorry about this."

Tracy nods. "Excuse me, I need some tissue." Sam nods.

Sam sits in his car, making a call.

"Hello, Sterling County Sheriff's Department, how can I help you?"

"Hi, is Sheriff Clark available?"

"Who may I say is calling?"

"Sheriff Duff."

"One second."

"Sam, how the hell are you?"

"Fair to middlin'."

"What can I do ya for?"

"I'm over here at Theodore Hart's place, and I got a tidbit I think ya might like to know."

"Do tell."

"It seems Theodore was interested in this Billy, over there."

"Ah, that would be Billy Bates."

"Yeah, I think that's right. She didn't know any more than he was after Billy. That's what Theodore's lady told me."

"That's strange. He's the one that called in the body."

"Who?"

"Billy."

"He did?"

"Yep, him and his girlfriend Sylvia."

"Have ya locked the boy down? He may go rabbit on ya."

"With this piece of information, I guess I'm going to have to."

"Have ya determined the cause of death yet?"

"Yeah, yeah, he was hit in the forehead, probably stunned him, and then a blow to the base of the neck. Death by blunt force trauma. Maybe something like a piece of wood—most likely a baseball bat."

"I got some more info for ya. He injured his head when he wrecked his car —smacking his head on the steering wheel. She said his Caddy is in the shop there in Sterling City."

"Well, that's one mystery solved. You say his car is in the shop here?"

"Yeah, yellow Caddy. I think it's a sixty-nine. But don't quote me on that. He took real good care of that car."

"You're full of all kinds of good information."

"And let me guess, ya haven't found a bat?"

"You got it. But we did find a gun. It seems not to belong to anyone."

"Oh, one more thing: he was traveling around in a truck. I guess he borrowed it from Old Man Jenkins."

"A truck. I wonder what happened to the truck?"

"Maybe he was killed somewhere else? Dumped there maybe?"
"Now there's a thought."

Thirteen
If I Could Read Your Mind

Ann leans against the desk, staring off, listening to the private investigator.

"It's like he fell off the face of the earth," he says.

"How does someone do that—especially him?" Ann replies.

"I'll keep looking, but it's not looking good. You know I've done a lot of work for you, but I've never seen anything like this. Is it possible someone killed him?"

"God, I don't even want to go there."

"I'll keep at it. If he's alive and kicking out there, he'll show up."

"Okay, thanks." Ann shuts her phone, staring off.

"What did he say?" Lester asks. They lock eyes.

"Oh, he can't find him."

"Do you think something happened to him?"

"That's what he was wondering. I don't know. It's pretty hard for him to hide. I know, I've been with him. He attracts a lot of attention everywhere he goes."

"I'll get on some chat boards and see if anything pops up."

"I think I'll go back to Texas. It's silly staying here thinking something is going to change."

"Okay. If anything pops up, I'll contact you."

Don and Jim look over the lobby of the County Seat of Sterling County.

"Hey, Sheriff, we got two Texas Rangers here."

"Okay, send 'em back."

The deputy directs Jim and Don to Sheriff Martin Clark's office. They pop their heads in.

"How the hell are you two?" Martin says.

"Doin' good," Don replies. Jim tips his hat.

"How can I help ya fellas?"

"We see a Billy Bates popped up on a death y'all had recently?"

"Word travels fast. Yeah, he reported a death. Him and his girlfriend. The body was found at her place."

"Would that be Sylvia?" Don asks.

"Do you boys know these two?"

"We do."

"Is that right—on shoot, that's right, y'all worked the Little John case."

"We did."

"Right, right."

"And the victim was Theodore Hart?"

"Yep. That's right."

"And that's Brett Hart's cousin."

"You boys seem to know a lot about our little town."

"A little," Jim replies. "Where was the body found?"

"In front of the barn. It was blunt force trauma."

Jim glances at Don. "I'll be," they echo.

"What?"

"Your Little John also had a blow to the head," Don says.

"That's right," Martin remarks. "Now that ya mention it, I remember reading the report."

"Have ya talked to Brett Hart yet?"

"Yep, in fact, I just got back from his place."

"Any help?"

"Actually, it was confusing," Martin replies.

"How so?"

"He said his cousin stabbed him with an ice pick and stole the gun."

"An ice pick?"

"Yeah. I guess he attacked him twice, two separate times, stabbing him once in the leg and another time in the arm. Nasty shit. I did pull an ice pick off the victim. Anyway, that's his explanation for how the gun got in the barn."

"Ice pick, Jesus."

"Yeah."

"Ya got a handle on who killed him?"

"Not sure. It seems he wasn't much liked. This case really stinks. Theodore was stalking Sylvia—at least that's what she says. And, I got a call from Sheriff Duff, over in Big Springs, and he said Theodore was after Billy."

"Billy," Jim remarks.

"What ya got on Billy?" Martin asks.

"Nothing, except he keeps popping up in our investigations—he seems to be a hub. What do ya know about Billy?"

"A lot. Kind of a quiet guy. He hung out with Little John—they were best friends. And he sees Sylvia. He's never really caused any problems."

"Billy's mom thinks Sylvia is after Billy's house."

"Oh, Peggy is always thinking something. She likes to gossip. Sylvia already has a house."

"She sure has opinions. Anything else?"

"The oddest thing—there was no vehicle found."

"Maybe he parked and walked in?"

"Yep, but nothing. We looked all the way up to The Cue Ball."

"The Cue Ball," Don remarks.

"Ya know it?"

"In our investigation into Little John, it seemed to be another hub of where all these people hang out."

"There seems to be a lot of hubs with you fellas?"

"Maybe. Okay, how about orbit?" Jim suggests.

"Okay. Whatever. Look, I'm headed to The Cue Ball now to talk with one of the bartenders, Tim Lucas. How would you boys like to tag along?" Jim and Don look at each other and nod.

The officers enter The Cue Ball. It's mid-afternoon and business is light. A couple of people sit at the bar. Tim leans against the counter, reading a newspaper. Seeing the officers, he snaps into action.

"Hello gentleman, how may I help you?"

"Hi Tim, I wanted to talk to you about the situation over at Sylvia's."

"Okay, Sheriff. I don't know if I can help. I mean, I wasn't there, but I'll try."

"Good enough. Sylvia said you chased the victim out of here that night? Have I got that right?"

"Yeah, yeah. It was the second time he'd been here within the week. He was asking a lot of questions about Billy and Sylvia the first time, and then he shows up and is staring down Sylvia—very creepy. I think he was stalking her. She certainly had his attention."

"How do you know that?"

"Like I said, he was watching her, and I had this feeling about him, so I said to Sylvia that she might want to take off early, so when she left, he tried to follow her. I planted my bat in his chest, stopping him, asking him to leave."

"What do ya mean by planted?"

"Ya know, like I put it out like this." Tim gestures. "Placing it in the middle of his chest—maybe 'placing' is a better word. I didn't hit him with it, or anything like that."

"I see. A bat, you say? Was there anything unusual about him?"

"Unusual . . . Oh yeah, he had this big knot on his forehead. Here's the bat." Tim pulls the bat out from underneath the bar for the officers to inspect.

"I see," Martin remarks, looking over the bat. "A knot, you say?" Don and Jim give the bat a good look.

"Yeah, big nasty one."

"And he left?"

"He did."

"Did you follow him outside?"

"Nah, it was crazy busy, and Sylvia left, so I was tending bar all alone."

"Did he come back?"

"Not that I saw."

Don hands the bat back to Tim.

"So did this bat ever go missing?"

"What, like ever? Or that night?"

"That night."

"Not that I know. But like I said, it was really busy. I didn't get out of here until three."

The Rangers sit in their SUV, digesting what they'd heard.

"Whatcha thinkin'?" Don asks.

"I'm thinkin' Billy and Brett keep popping up."

"Yeah . . . Let's go look at the crime scene."

"Okay, but one thing before we go. What happened to Sylvia?"

"Whatcha talkin' about?"

"She left early. Did she drive home, walk? How did she hook up with Billy?"

"I see. What's her address?"

"It's 514 Hiler. It looks like it's at the end of Main Street here."

"If that's true, we can try to trace her movement that night."

Tim's head whips around as he monitors the bar. He has the handset to his ear.

"Hello."

"Dude, the Sheriff was here with two Texas Rangers."

"What?"

"Yeah, man."

"Rangers? Damn, I've met those guys before," Brett says.

"Ya have?"

"Yeah, at The Cue Ball. They were looking for Billy, but then they started crawling up my ass. Shit."

"They seem to be focused on Sylvia and Billy."

"But Skinny's my cousin."

"Yeah. I know. I wanted to give you a heads up."

Don eases the SUV into the clearing at Sylvia's place. They do a visual survey of the area.

"Look at that. An old chicken coop," Don says. The two slip out of the SUV.

"Hear that?" Jim asks. Don focuses on the sounds.

"It's quiet."

"Yeah, no dogs barking."

"You're right," Don replies, swinging his head. "Also, it's very secluded. Have ya got the photos?"

"Oh shoot." Jim goes back into the SUV, pulling out a folder. He shoulders up with Don. Jim pulls the photos out; they both look at the barn.

"Okay," Don points. "If he landed here, face down, whoever was waiting for him most likely waited for him right there."

"Right." Jim moves to the barn doors. "Which means he came out of the barn." Jim grabs one door, and Don the other, swinging them open. They both look at an empty barn.

"Why would he go in here?" Don whips his head toward the house. "If he was stalking her, why wouldn't he be in the backyard? You know, lurking behind one of these trees? There are plenty of big trees to hide behind."

"Surprise, maybe?"

"Maybe? Look at all that real estate between here and the backdoor. Kinda odd, wouldn't you say?"

"Where was the gun found?" Don asks. Jim looks at the photo and points.

"It looks like that second stall to the left." They walk to the stall.

"Okay, so he takes Brett's gun and leaves it here—"

"Nah, he lost it. It says here it was found partially found under the hay."

"Was there a fight?"

"Could have been. Whatcha thinking?"

"How about this—Billy, or Brett found him in here, they fought, he lost the gun, ran out and the other one was waiting to whack him."

Jim strokes his chin. "Let's say that's true—why would he go in here?"

"Do ya think he was waiting here?"

"I'm going to guess, yes."

"What would compel him to run out of the barn?"

"Hard to say?"

"The Cue Ball is not too far from here. Do ya think he walked here?"

"Maybe? It would explain why there was no vehicle found."

"Right, right." They move to the opening, looking at the house.

"Okay, so you're him. Let's say you're in that stall. What would cause you to run out of this barn?"

"You're either chased or threatened?"

"You're chased out of here to someone waiting to whack you on the head?"

"A tag team? We're back to Billy and Brett working together."

"I guess we are?"

"What about Billy and Sylvia? They did call in the body."

"Maybe? But I was thinking more about Billy and Brett."

"And Sylvia was a spectator?"

"That's a good question."

"Do we take over?"

"Not yet. Let's let the Sheriff work it awhile longer before we pull rank. I do think we should talk to Brett. It was his gun found here after all."

Ann's depression deepens. She spends more time in bed these days. *C'mon Ann, get up. I know. Maybe later? This is not good for you. I know. Maybe in a minute?* Ann rolls over, pulling the covers over her head. Her phone rings. She pops out from underneath the blankets. *C'mon, answer it. Oh—*

"Hello."

"How ya doing, hon?"

"Kay?"

"Who else would it be?"

"I don't know? I don't care."

"You don't care? What—"

"I'm sorry. That sounded bad."

"It sure did. Still no word on Tom?"

"It's like he's been vaporized. Even my PI can't find him—believe me, if he can't find him, no one can."

"That's not good. Look, I'm worried about you. Are you in bed?"

"No."

"Ann."

"Okay, so what?"

"You need to get out. I'm coming up there. Meet me for coffee."

"I don't know."

"Ann."

"Okay, Mom."

"You're funny. Meet me at that cute place—"

"The Coffeehouse?"

"That's the one."

"Okay."

"And, Ann."

"Yeah."

"Show up this time."

Tom smells the bacon. His stomach growls. There's a knock at the door. Tom draws the blanket over his shoulder. There's another knock. He rolls over on his side.

"Tom . . . Tom." There's another knock. "Tom, I have breakfast." There's another knock. "Tom, you need to get up." Tom throws the blankets back.

"Okay, I'll be there in a second." Tom sits up, putting his feet on the floor. He rubs his face. He combs his fingers through his hair. He slides into his pants and drapes a shirt over his body. Barefooted, he stumbles through the hall to the kitchen. A plate of bacon and eggs is waiting.

"There you are," Ester remarks.

"Morning."

Ester carries her plate, joining him.

"Good morning. Have you thought about what we talked about last night?"

"Lately, all I do is think."

"Have you thought about how long you're going to hide out here?"

"You want me to go—"

"No, no. I'm thinking, maybe, it's time to make a plan—I think it would be good for your mental state."

Tom shovels through his meal. "Man, this is good."

"Depression is a wicked dance partner."

"What do you mean?"

"You've wallowed in your pain, which has been necessary, but if you stay there too long, you'll never come back. It has been wonderful having you here, but I'm worried about you."

"I worry. I worry about what an asshole I've been."

"Look, you can beat yourself up all you want, but at some point, don't you wonder what the point is? I think you should plan something, anything. It doesn't matter what it is, but you have to snap out of this. It's time."

"Plan something?"

"Yeah. You need to do something else—besides wandering through the house."

"But we've been talking. I know I don't act like it, but it's helping. And I really needed this break. I thank you so much for opening your home."

"I know you feel awful about Kathy, but Tom, you didn't pull the trigger. No matter how much blame you want to take on, you didn't pull the trigger."

"I know. But I feel like I might as well have."

"C'mon, I'll help you. Let's plan something."

"I keep seeing Kathy sitting in that chair. That vacant look."

"That's the point. We need to get you to focus on something else."

"But it haunts me."

"Exactly. We need to get your brain working on something else."

"Yeah, I guess you're right."

Don knocks a second time. Jim surveys the neighborhood. They share a glance.

"Didn't the Sheriff say he just talked with him?" Jim asks.

"As far as I recall. Why don't you go snoop in the back?"

"Okay." Jim walks with purpose, making it to the back gate. He opens the gate and surveys the backyard. Seeing the back garage door, he decides to peek through the window. *No vehicle. I'd say this boy is gone.* He moves to the sliding glass door, giving the handle a yank; it doesn't budge. He returns to Jim.

"There's no vehicle in the garage."

"I was afraid you were going to tell me that."

A horn honks. Tom pulls the curtain back, peeking. The taxi waits. He looks for anyone that might be waiting for him. It looks safe. He puts on his hat and sunglasses. He makes a dash for the taxi, hopping in the back.

"William?" the driver asks.

"Ahh, yeah."

"How's your day going?"

"Good. And you?"

"Good. Where to?"

"The airport to rent a car."

"Which one?"

"Alamo."

"Okay, you got it. Sit back and relax and I'll have you there in no time."

"Thanks."

The Rangers enter Sheriff Clark's office.

"How you two doing?" Martin asks.

"Good," they echo.

"We were out at Brett Hart's place, and he's not there. Is he working? We thought you were out there earlier today?" Jim asks.

"Yep, I was. He's most likely working. Hey, I got something you two might be interested in. Let's head down the hall."

The Sheriff leads the Rangers into a room.

"Ya going to be questioning someone?" Don asks. They all gaze through a mirror into an interrogation room.

"Were bringing in Billy Bates," Martin replies.

Deputy Jerry escorts Billy down a long hall. He unlocks the door, pulling it open. Billy peeks into an interrogation room.

"Oh, shit," Billy remarks.

"Sorry about this, Billy. Sheriff Clark says he wants to have a chat."

Billy hesitates. "Why here? Can't I talk to him in his office?"

"I don't know. I do what I'm told." Jerry leads him inside. "You can sit there," Jerry says, pointing.

"Damn, okay."

Jerry exits. Billy stares at the mirror. *Isn't this dandy? I knew I should have gotten rid of Skinny's body.* He fidgets in his seat. *Man, this feels too much like Chicago, which means I'm a suspect. Damn, I should have gotten rid of the body.* Martin and the Rangers watch through the mirror.

"What you fellas think?" Martin asks.

"He does seem to be at the center of this thing," Don replies.

"I brought him in because of what you fellas were saying. I've known Billy since he was a little tike. He's done a little mischief, nothing too bad."

"I understand, Sheriff," Jim says. "You know about Billy and Little John?"

"Sure."

"Okay, so hang with me here. Little John beat the crap out of that coach a while back, and he took off for the border. Now something happened, he changed his mind or something, but anyway, you know, he died. And then Billy runs over the coach's assistant, Pete—in Chicago? There's got to be a connection," Don says.

"We're not sure what it is—but Skinny and Pete were best friends," Jim remarks. "I mean, how many times has Billy been to Chicago?"

"I'm not sure on that one. But if I had to guess, I don't think ever? If he did, he never talked about it."

"Okay, so what are the odds, his only trip to Chicago, he happens to run over a guy from Big Springs?" Jim says.

"And now Pete's best friend is found dead at his girlfriend's house," Don remarks.

"Okay, I get it. I don't see Billy as a killer."

"Let's see what he says?"

"Okay." Martin watches as the Rangers pay a visit to Billy.

The door opens. Billy's head snaps to the door. The Rangers enter. *Crap. Not these two.* Billy slumps in his chair.

"Hi Billy," Don says.

"You two."

"That's right," Jim replies.

"Where's Sheriff Clark? I was told I would be talking to the Sheriff."

"He'll be along shortly," Don remarks. "Billy, you've been a busy guy."

"How so?"

"Ya know, Chicago."

"And now this Skinny guy," Jim remarks.

"I didn't kill Skinny."

"Now, Billy, did we say that? What makes you talk like that, son?"

"Because I'm in this room."

"Now ya know why we have these rooms?"

"To fuck with people?"

"Funny," Jim says, looking at Don. "You're a funny guy. Billy, anyone ever tell you you're a funny guy?"

"Not recently." Billy folds his arms.

"No, it's about distractions. There's no phones, or people interrupting. It's just us, talkin'."

"Isn't that dandy?"

"C'mon, help us out here, and then we can send you on your way," Jim says. Billy shrugs.

"Do you know, or maybe I should say, did you know Skinny?" Don asks.

"Yeah, so?"

"And you have had some kind of run in with him?"

"Not really, but he was stalking Sylvia."

"But ya know who he is?" Don asks.

"Yeah, he's Brett's cousin."

"Very good," Jim replies. "He's also the best friend of Pete, that guy you ran over in Chicago."

"He was?"

"C'mon Billy, you didn't know that?"

"No, no I didn't."

"Huh," Don remarks. "Kinda crazy, don't ya think? You at the death of both fellas, and they happened to be best friends and all?"

"Yeah. Crazy."

"Tell us, why'd ya go to Chicago?" Jim asks. Billy glares at the agents. He knew someday someone might ask, but the question still caught him off guard. Behind the mirror, deputy Jerry Green enters. Martin gives him a glance. Jerry shoulders up with Martin, watching the Rangers work Billy.

"We gotta match for the gun," Jerry says.

"And?"

"It does indeed belong to Brett Hart, and it was shot."

Martin's head snaps, locking eyes with Jerry.

"Yeah, Brett said it went off when he struggled with Skinny."

"And Skinny's fingerprints were the only ones found on the gun."

"Right."

"Sure, makes ya wonder. A guy gets whacked in the head, and a few feet away was a gun."

They watch the Rangers. "Do ya think he borrowed it from Brett?"

"Nah, Brett said he took it."

"Took it." They watch the Rangers.

"Yeah, something about an ice pick to the shoulder."

"Oh shoot, he was shot."

They lock eyes. "What? I didn't see any gunshot wound."

"It was old. He was patched up on his left shoulder. He was shot with a shotgun."

"It seems this Skinny was a busy beaver." They watch the Rangers.

Jim asks, "Billy, was Skinny really stalking your girlfriend?"

"Or was he stalking you?" Don asks. Billy is silent.

"Try this one out, Billy. Skinny was after you. You slipped him, and for some reason, he thinks you're at Sylvia's. You double back and whack him. Hell, maybe you were using Sylvia as a decoy?"

"No, no, no. I was as surprised as you that he ended up dead on Sylvia's land. Let's say I was going to do this—why would I do it at Sylvia's place? And then call it in?"

"Now, you do have a point there. I don't know, maybe to throw people off your scent?"

Fourteen
The Long and Winding Road

Tom drives the streets of Big Springs—the memories assault him. Turning onto his street, the neighborhood looks the same; things in Big Springs don't change much. Tom eases into the driveway behind his truck. *My truck? What's my truck doing here?* Because the truck garners the attention, he misses the new lawn. Out of the car, he circles the truck—gawking. *You've got to be kidding?* He gives special attention to damaged areas, at least the ones he can remember. *No dents, no broken glass—Huh. It's even been washed—It looks great.* Flashing back on that night—the night he planted the truck in the middle of his yard, mowing down the For Sale sign—smashing the headlight, and damaging the bumper. He caresses the bumper. *Who fixed it? It looks new.* Twisting toward the house, the new lawn catches his eye. *A new lawn too? Cut, trimmed, and green. Who's been taking care of the place?* He steps on the turf. *Huh.* He stomps on it; the same exercise he would do before his teams played on a newly sodded field. *It's firm. It's been here a while.* On guard, he creeps across the yard, inspecting for any other changes. *No little wood spears, no signpost, no sign. It's all gone and cleaned up.* On the porch, he peeks behind the hedge, looking for glass fragments. *All that's cleaned up too—interesting. I have to say, the place looks great.* Kathy always described the house as a *shithole*, but in fact, it was one of the largest and nicest houses in Big Springs.

He slides the key into the lock. Stopping, he spins, giving the yard another glance. He didn't imagine it. *Wow.* He pushes open the door. The inside looks the same, except for the new layer of dust. It's so strange when you know a space so well, and then once you've been away, it seems foreign—like the lamp—he's turned that lamp on hundreds of times, but he grapples to find the switch. *Let there be light.* His eyes lock on it. *Damn, that brick.* He slides the easy chair aside, gripping the brick, wrestling with it. Dislodging it, he inspects it. *It's not broken or chipped. So odd. Why hasn't anyone removed it? I would have thought they would have needed it for evidence. Huh, I guess not.* He places it on the end table. Bending down, he inspects the damage to the wall, gazing at the hole. *That shouldn't be a big deal to fix—Should it? Not that I've ever fixed a hole in a wall before. I'm assuming it won't be hard to fix.*

Standing, he turns his attention to the rest of the house. Drifting from room to room, he notices all Kathy's and the kids' things are gone. He flashes on Mooresville. *The boxes.* He replays Pete's truck sliding to a stop—the gunfire. He shivers. *God, this stuff is going to haunt me forever. Where's the mail? They must have stopped delivery.* His tour of the house takes him back to the living room. Giving one final survey, he thinks, *Okay, time to move on.* He collects the brick.

Standing on Cindy's front porch, Tom raps on the door. Herb answers.

"Tom, is that you?"

"Hi, Herb."

"How the hell are ya?"

"Good, I guess?"

"Are ya back?"

"Kinda."

"Are you coaching next season? That's what I heard—I mean, that's what they're saying? Hell I—"

"Nah. I'm cleaning up some stuff."

"Oh. I get it—I do—really."

"Herb, it's okay. Is Cindy here?"

"Sure. Come on inside."

"Thanks." Tom enters.

"Have a seat. I'll fetch her." Tom nods while he sits on the couch.

Cindy enters. Tom stands.

"Tom." They hug. "What are you doing here?"

"Housekeeping."

"They cleaned up your house, ya know. Have you been there? It sure looks dandy."

"I have. And it does—it looks amazing."

"I think the whole town helped clean it up."

"The outside, at least," Tom remarks.

"Oh, ya went inside?"

"Yeah. I harvested the brick."

"Oh, that brick. It gives me chills just hearing about it."

"I can't believe it's been lodged in there all this time. Listen, I want you to sell my house. You still do that, right?"

"Ah, yeah, sure."

"There's a big hole in the wall where I pulled the brick out, so that needs to be fixed. Anyway, go through it. Anything you think needs repaired or fixed, go ahead and have it done."

"All right. Are you guys really leaving?"

"It's time to move on."

"Okay, you got it. I went up and saw Kathy." Tom's face contorts. "Oh, I'm sorry, I think I upset you?"

He stares down. "I feel awful."

"I get it. Not another word."

"Are there some papers I need to sign?"

"Sure. I'll be right back."

"And is there any chance you can call Paul for me?"

"Sure. Herb."

Tom eases the car in front of Burt's. He peers into the big picture window; Burt and Paul sit in barber's chairs, jawing away. He sighs. Grabbing the brick, he heads into Burt's.

"Tom," Burt says. "So good to see ya." Paul stands—they shake.

"How ya been, Tom?" Paul asks.

"Good, well, better. How are things here?"

"We're glad to see you," Burt remarks. "Have ya seen your place? It's looking spiffy. We're excited about ya returning to coach the Steers next year."

"Here, Tom, I got the keys to your truck." Paul dangles a key chain.

"You did that?"

"The whole town did. We did a little fundraiser."

"Ah."

"What ya got there?" Burt asks.

"I got a present for you, Burt." Tom holds out the brick. Burt is not sure what to do—he takes it.

"A brick?" Burt chuckles as he inspects it. "This is the damnedest present I've ever gotten. What's on it—chalk?"

"Drywall."

"What you say?"

"You know, from my house."

"Oh shoot. Is this that—"

"Yep."

"Now Tom, I never—"

"Think of it as a reminder."

"A reminder, you say?"

"Yeah, the next time ya want to, oh hell, how do I say this? You want to kinda push things."

"I'm not following."

"So that's—" Paul interjects. They lock eyes. Tom nods.

"Yep."

"Now, Tom, I feel awful about—"

Tom smiles. "Uh-huh."

"Really, Tom. I'm real sorry about what happened that night."

"I know. Let this be a reminder—for the next time you're cooking up something."

"Oh."

"I suggest you put it someplace where you can see it—you know, so you don't forget."

"Okay, real good then. Thank you," Burt says. Tom nods, smiling.

"I got the call from Herb. What's up?" Paul asks.

"I thought you two should know. I put the house up for sale."

"For sale? You're not coming back?" Burt asks.

"No. I'd turn this place into a circus. It looks like my coaching days are over. Believe me when I say this: I'm saving you all. I got these people, some call them my flock, who think I'm the *one* or some bullshit like that."

"The one for what?" Burt asks.

"Exactly. Anyway, they're really good at tracking me down. And then there's the media—although, I haven't had much of an issue with them lately."

"Hell, son, this is great news. That's more ticket sales," Burt remarks.

"I guess that's one way to look at it?"

"Is that why y'all are wearing the hat and sunglasses?" Burt asks.

"Yep. I'm kinda incognito. I've been off the grid for a while, which is why I would like you to keep our little meeting private. I thought doing this in person would be best."

"I appreciate that, Tom," Paul says. "It's so sad to see you go."

"Yeah, I know, but it is what it is. I'm sure someone will come snooping around. If you would tell them, can you tell them I'm headed to Ann's."

"Is that the pretty nurse?" Burt asks.

"Yep."

"Ya know, she was in here not too far back. Wow, Tom, what a looker."

Tom smiles. "She is that."

"How's Kathy?" Paul asks.

"I'd rather not talk about that."

"I understand. We're sorry to see ya go, but you made at least one person's day."

"I did?"

"Yeah, I got this young man who's been filling in for ya at school—you know, covering your classes. I can now tell him he's going to be permanent."

"Who the hell is going to coach the team?" Burt asks.

"We'll figure it out," Paul replies.

"I got a name for you," Tom remarks.

"Ya do?"

"Yeah, JR."

"JR," Burt looks at Paul.

"That might work," Paul replies.

"Where ya headed to now?" Burt asks.

"Not exactly sure."

Ann's back in bed. It's mid-afternoon. Her phone rings; she doesn't look at the number. The only one that calls these days is Kay.

"Hi, Kay. Yes, I'm in bed."

There's throat clearing. "Ms. Collins?"

She sits up. "Yes."

"Hi, this is Beaks."

"I'm so sorry—"

"No problem. I have an update—Mr. Thompson has popped up."

"He has?"

"Yes. He rented a car at the Cleveland Hopkins Airport."

"A car? When?"

"Two days ago."

"Have you got a clue where he's headed?"

"Looks like, according to the info he gave them at the counter, he went to Chicago."

"Chicago. Okay." Like she's thinking out loud. "Why Chicago?"

"I don't know, ma'am. He made a large ATM withdrawal close to the airport. I've been trying to track him to Chicago, but I haven't come up with anything—at least not yet. Anyway, that's my update."

"Oh, thank you. Really."

"Anytime."

Ann sits, pondering. She calls Kay.

"What happened?" Kay answers.

"How do you know something happened?"

"You're calling me."

"Oh." Ann laughs.

"And we're laughing. This must be good news?"

"Yep. Tom popped up. He rented a car and is headed to Chicago."

"I don't get it. Why would he be going to Chicago?"

"Yeah, why would *he* be going to Chicago?"

Tom drives past the service station; the one where his tire got poked the night of the coin-toss. Straining to see, he's wondering if the attendant is working. He's traveling too fast to get a good look. *Wow, the last time I was on this stretch of road, I was doing a hundred and ten. God, that seems like another lifetime. Actually, it was another life.* He flashes back on trying to work the radio. *Jesus, I could have killed myself. Yeah, sometimes I do stupid shit.*

He is so lost in reminiscing that he is surprised that The Truck Stop is off to the right. *Wow, that was fast.* He turns, passing a sign that reads: *The Place Coach Thompson Died. Tours Inside.* There's an arrow pointing to the restaurant. *You gotta be kidding.* Tom eases into an empty parking slot. A group of people surround the pole—that pole—the one where he went into a coma. One person is talking, arms flailing, pointing out details. The spectators watch. *I'll be damned. You'd think after what I've been through, nothing would surprise me. Maybe I should sneak out and scare the hell out of them?* He chuckles. Tom observes for a moment before driving on.

The Coffeehouse became the go-to place for Ann and Kay to get together. Kay watches Ann, who is on the phone.

"What does that mean?" Ann asks.

"I'm not sure?" Beaks remarks. "He's working really hard not to be found. I can tell you this, he's not in Chicago."

"Okay, thanks."

Ann and Kay lock eyes.

"Not good," Kay remarks.

"No. Damn, where is he? Now he's surfaced, but still, one way can track him."

"You two did get a lot of practice slipping people."

"I guess." Ann's eyes well up.

"Maybe he's doing something for himself?"

"Like what?" Ann cries.

"Oh, hon, I'm sorry."

"Shit. I thought we had something—ya know?"

"I know."

"Why doesn't he call me and tell me what's going on?" Ann grabs a tissue, wipes her eyes, blowing her nose. "Dammit. I thought he was the one. Dammit, Thomas, where are you?"

Tom feels better as he glances at the countryside. So far, it's been a great trip; no media, no groupies, no real destination—healing for the soul. It's like the clouds are parting. *Ester was right, again. Man, that woman is always right.* When the trip started, Tom was on constant guard, looking, watching; basically, paranoid that he was being followed. He quit looking long ago. He passes the sign for Brownsville. *Wow, already at the border. Interesting how the miles fly by when ya got nowhere to go.*

He passes a sign for a diner; his stomach gurgles. *What is this, the power of suggestion?* He pulls into a slot up front. Collecting a few things, like his cash, he glances into the mirror, checking his hat. Satisfied, he gets out. *It feels good to stretch the legs.* Inside, a pleasant man greets him.

"Howdy, sit anywhere you like."

Tom nods. *That corner booth looks good.* Max follows with a coffee pot in hand.

"How ya doin' today?" Max asks.

Tom settles in. "Good. How about you?"

"I'm doing dandy. Coffee?"

"Sure."

"Room for cream?"

"Nah, I'll take it black."

"Okay then," Max pours the coffee. "The menu is right there," Max says, pointing. "In the rack to your right. I'll be back."

"Okay, thanks."

Tom snatches a menu. He removes his hat and sunglasses, massaging his head, combing his fingers through his hair. *Man, that feels better.* Life is all about timing, and at this moment, Max catches a full glimpse of Tom's face.

"I'll be," Max mumbles. Making his way back to Tom's table, Max slips into the booth, sitting opposite of Tom.

Tom jumps. "You scared the crap out of me." Tom catches his breath.

"Sorry, I didn't mean to scare you." Max's eyes narrow. "You're him? Aren't ya? You're that coach?"

"Shit." Tom slaps the hat and glasses back on.

"It's okay, I won't give you up."

"You won't?"

"Hell no." Max grins. "Ya want to hear something crazy?"

"How crazy?"

"Crazy. This is some really crazy shit."

"Okay. What?"

Max points. "The big fella sat right there."

"Big fella?"

"Yeah. The one they reported that killed you. Ya know, before ya did your Jesus thing," Max says, beaming.

"Here?" Tom looks, swiveling his head like the booth is going to swallow him up.

"Right there. That very spot."

"Jesus. Really?"

"Yep. Crazy, isn't it?"

"That's crazy, all right. He was here?"

"Yep. I think he was going to cross the border. He was burdened with a heavy heart. Ya could tell that. We get folks in here from time to time who are thinking about crossing, ya know, something bad happened ta 'em, ya know."

"But he died in San Antonio, didn't he?"

"Yep. He did. He must have changed his mind. You could tell he was a troubled soul. I didn't know then but often thought later, it was about you."

"Me. You're right, that's some crazy shit." Tom glances out the window.

"I'm beginning to wonder, ya know, if that spot collects souls who are troubled? Ya know, like some kind of vortex."

Tom stares at Max. "Are you saying I looked troubled?"

"Well—aren't ya?"

"Yeah, I suppose I am."

"Ya see?"

"Uh-huh. How did you pick me out so fast? I had my glasses—"

"I know all about your adventures. I've become like an expert on you."

"You have?"

"Yep. After we figured out who the big guy was, you two became my hobby. I think I've followed everything about you—hell, I've seen you so many times on TV, in the paper. Heck, I might know more about you than you."

Tom chuckles. "You probably do. I can't remember much about that night. I remember looking into this truck, and nothing else."

"Yeah, that wasn't a good night for ya. And that awful thing in Mooresville. Hell son, it seems a dark cloud has been pissing on your life for a while."

"That's one way to put it."

"Kinda like Jesus, don't ya think?"

"What?"

"Yeah, he went through all these trials, ya know, to test him."

"You think I'm being tested? Like Jesus?"

"Maybe."

"I don't know too much about Jesus."

"And yet—"

"I get what you're driving at. I've been looking at it as a bunch of bad shit happening to me, and the people around are getting caught up in it. I've been thinking they would be better off if I went it alone."

"That's not much of a life, is it? Going it alone? Maybe ya need to heal some?"

"I feel great. Better than I have in years."

"That's not the healing I'm talkin' about. The inside." Max points to his heart. "This is something better served with time behind it."

"What?"

"Ya know, perspective."

Tom stares out the window. "I guess."

"Ya sound adrift."

"You have no idea."

"Are you telling me it's all been bad?" They lock eyes.

"No. I can't say that." Tom flashes on Ann.

"My mama always told me to count your blessings along the way."

"That is a good one. It's not that easy sometimes. I get what you're driving at though. Your mama sounds like a wise woman."

"She was that. Funny, the older I get, the more I understand that."

"Yeah, life is strange."

"Sure is. Ya know, following you has been better than any movie or TV show."

"It's a little different on this side of the table—you know, living it."

"Yeah, a suppose it is. Ya think they'll make a movie about you?"

Tom chuckles. "Who knows? Probably."

"It's a damn fascinating story."

"Unless you're the one living it." Tom gives a blank stare. "Back to the big fella. You say you think he wanted to cross the border?"

"Yep, I'm pretty sure. Let's put it this way—I was surprised when he didn't."

"Are you like an expert on crossing?"

"Heck, I don't know about that."

"Do you need a passport to get across?"

"Are your groupies wearin' ya out?"

"You know about them?

"I told ya, you've become my hobby," Max remarks.

"Huh."

"Anyway, you can cross—that's pretty easy. It's the getting back. You'll need a passport or birth certificate. I've heard of a few people getting back with a driver's license—but I think they had to bribe their way back in."

"Okay, thanks for the info."

"Are ya crossing?"

"I don't know. I guess I'm collecting information right now?"

Max stands. "Can I throw in a penny's worth of advice?"

"Sure, why not?"

"You can hate your life, which will bring you a mountain load of misery. But as far as my experience goes, life is like the weather—ya wait long enough—it will change."

"You're a wise man."

"I have my moments. Ya ready to order?"

"Give me a second."

"Okay, you got it." Max stands.

The door opens. Brett Hart limps in, standing at the door, waiting. Max yells.

"Howdy, sit anywhere ya like."

Brett nods, grabbing a seat at the counter.

Fifteen

The Call

Sheriff Clark and the Rangers are on a mission, searching for Brett. They've checked his house, his work, Billy's, Sylvia's. They're now at The Cue Ball.

"Hi, Tim."

"Hi, Sheriff."

"Hey, we're looking for Brett. Have ya seen him lately?"

"Did he do something?"

"We want to have a chat."

Tim ponders. "I think the last time he was in here was a few days ago?"

"I see. The boy seems to have fallen off the face of the earth."

"You think he's making a run for it?" Don asks.

"You think he's running?" Martin asks.

Don shrugs. "Just a thought."

The officers lock eyes on Tim like he's got Brett hidden.

Tim, glass-eyed, shrugs. "Don't look at me. I don't know."

Ann and Kay peruse the menu at a small cafe. They sit at a window table. Ann lowers the menu, gazing out the window, lost in thought. She tosses the menu to the table.

"I'm not hungry."

"Eating is not the point," Kay remarks.

"I know. Thanks for getting me out."

"Hon, I've been there. It's dangerous to lock yourself up in your home. You need light, air, company."

"You're right. Just getting dressed, putting on some makeup—I feel so much better. Being alone with my thoughts—" Her phone rings. "It's Lester." Kay nods. "Hello."

"Hi Ann, it's Lester."

"Hi Lester, how are you?"

"Good, I'm doing good. Hey, I got a tip. I don't know how good it is. Tom has been spotted in Big Springs." Ann perks up.

"Really?"

"Like I say, I'm not sure how good the info is, but that's what is flying around the chat board."

"I guess any news is good news, right?

"I guess.

"Thanks for the updated."

"Of course."

"Okay, thank you so much."

"You got it."

"What, what?" Kay asks.

"Finally, Tom has emerged. He's been seen in Big Springs."

"Are you shitting me?"

Ann smiles. "You up for a road trip?"

Kay smiles. "Sure, let me call and get someone to take my shift."

Brett sits, looking out the big picture window of M&H Auto Sales. The sign out front stated *Cash for Cars*. Brett always wondered about places that stated *Cash for Cars*. Did they really mean it? He took a chance. The salesman returns. Brett sits up straight.

"Okay, we ran your plate and registration on your truck. It all matches and looks clean. My guy did an appraisal, so the only question left is, how much do you want?"

"What's it worth?"

"My man tells me fifteen thousand. My manager said we can give you seven."

"Seven?" Brett mulls over the price. "How about eight?"

"Eight. I don't know. Tell you what, how about seven and a half?"

"Seven and a half." Brett studies his truck. "Okay, deal."

"You sure ya want it in cash? It's kinda dangerous running around with that much cash. I can have a cashier's check whipped up in a jiffy."

"Nah, I'd like the cash. That's why I'm giving ya such a great price."

"Cash it is. Give me a minute."

Brett waits, gazing out the window. The owner returns, placing a small envelope in front of Brett. Their eyes lock.

"Here ya go—count it. Once you're out that door, I can't help ya." Brett pulls out the bills, spreading them on the desk. Satisfied, he scoops the bills up, placing them back in the envelope, giving a nod. "Okay, sign right here and here. Once ya sign, it's a done deal and you can be on your way." Brett nods.

Brett stuffs the envelope in his backpack. What timing, the taxi pulls up. Brett slings the backpack over his shoulder and scurries to meet the cab. The driver lowers the window.

"You, Brett?"

Brett nods. "Yep."

"Hop in. How ya doin' today?" the driver asks.

Brett settles in. "Real fine, and you?"

"Can't complain. Where to?"

"The bus station."

"Okay, sit back and relax. I'll have you there shortly."

Brett closes his eyes, reflecting, reviewing his plan. *Okay, so that worked well.* He runs through his itinerary. *I wonder if they've figured it out yet? I've got a good jump on them, but is it enough?* His thoughts turn to the money. With the sale of his truck and the two cashier's checks, he has a tad over two hundred thousand dollars. The people at the bank squawked when he asked for the money in cash; something about how they needed a day to get that much in cash, so he took it in two cashier's checks. He left fifty thousand in his account so it wouldn't attract even more attention. Withdrawing that much money, in a place like Sterling City, is big news. It's not going to be long before he's the talk of the town.

Pulling into the bus terminal, Brett is ready to jump out. He slides a twenty to the cab driver for a $10.50 fare. The cabbie smiles when he doesn't want change. He stands, looking at the terminal. He sighs. *Okay, here we go.* He enters the bus terminal; it's bustling with activity. He scans the departure board. *There it is. The bus to San Fernando, departing at 11:45 am. Perfect.* He glances at his watch. It's 10:38 am. *Wow, I made it. This might work if I can buy a ticket without being arrested.* He steps up to the counter.

"Hi, I would like a ticket to San Fernando, Mexico."

"Do you need a return ticket?"

"No, I'm not sure how long I'll be down there."

"Okay, sir. That will be sixteen dollars, and I'll need your passport."

Brett slides his passport with the money on top through the little window. The man is having issues with his passport. Brett is trying to be calm—he's sweating. *Shit, what's the issue? Damn, damn, damn.* Trying to be discreet, his eyes wander for an escape route. *This sucks. I should run. RUN.* His legs won't move. It's like his feet are welded to the floor. The machine belches out a beep. The tension melts away as he relaxes. *Man, I almost blew it. Be cool, be cool. You got this.*

"Here you go, sir. Boarding is at gate four."

Brett grabs the change, ticket, and passport, giving an awkward smile. "How long is the bus ride?"

"About two hours."

He nods. "Okay, thanks." He stows the ticket away, slinging the backpack over his shoulder. He glances at the big clock. *The bus leaves at 11:45 plus two hours would put it roughly around 2:00. Cool.* He walks out front where the taxis are waiting. The first taxi in line lowers his window.

"Hi."

"Hi, I need to go to the marina."

"Okay, hop in." Brett settles into the back seat. "Which marina?"

"Pelican Point."

"You got it. Goin' fishin'?"

"Something like that."

Sheriff Clark and the Rangers stand on Billy's porch. It's their second visit in the last few hours. Martin knocks. Peggy answers.

"Hi, Peggy."

"Hi, back so soon?" She eyes the Rangers. "I see you're still runnin' around with those two." The Rangers tip their hats. "This must be trouble." Don and Jim share a smile.

"Is Billy here?"

"Nah, still not here. I told ya, he took off with that bitch in heat." The Rangers choke back a laugh. "I don't know where they went—I'm guessin' The Cue Ball?"

"No, we've just came from there."

"Okay then, I don't know where they went? He never tells me anything."

Martin's phone rings. "Okay, thanks, Peggy. Ya have a nice day." He answers the call. "Sheriff Clark."

"Hi, Martin. It's Sheriff Duff."

"Sam. What's up?"

"I got a call from Old Man Jenkins, and he is madder than a hornet. It seems his truck has been impounded over there in Sterling City. Theodore's lady told me they borrowed it. Judging on how mad Old Man Jenkins is, I'm guessin' without permission? Ya might want to check it out. I'm guessin' Skinny was the last one to drive it?"

"That's a twist. Thanks, Sam."

"Something break?" Jim asks.

"I think so. We need to talk to someone about a truck."

Ann and Kay pull in front of Tom's house; a *For Sale* sign is posted on the front lawn.

"Oh shit," Ann remarks.

"He's moving?"

"I'm guessing he's closing up loose ends."

"Cindy Willetts? I think that's the one that paid me a visit with those reporters."

Ann glances at the truck. "There's a truck here. I wonder if that's his truck? He said he had a truck."

"He must be here."

Ann lights up, smiling. "Maybe." Out of the car, they scoot to the porch. Ann knocks. They wait.

"It's awfully quiet," Kay remarks. Ann nods.

Ann pulls out her phone. The call goes to voice mail. "Hi, Tom. Kay and I are outside your house. We're on the front porch. Are you home?" Ann peeks through the picture window; the curtains are drawn. She twists, looking at the street. "Are you in there?"

"Voice mail?" Kay asks. Ann nods. "Maybe he's out back?"

"Maybe." They walk the property, popping into the backyard.

"This guy is good at hiding."

"Too good." They circle back to the car. "I think we need to see the barber?"

"The barber?"

"Yeah, the barber knows everything that goes on in this town. He might even tell us where this Cindy lives."

"Why? Let's just call her? Her numbers are right there. We could set up a showing."

"Isn't that brilliant?" Ann remarks. Kay has her phone to her ear, talking. She ends her call. "Well?"

"We got an appointment in thirty minutes."

"Brilliant. Let's get some coffee. If we're waiting when she pulls up, she might keep driving."

Ann and Kay return to Tom's house, pulling in behind Cindy's car. Cindy whistles in the kitchen. The door is open.

"I don't think she's going to be happy about this," Kay remarks.

"Now you're getting cold feet? This was your idea."

"I know. I'm just saying."

"Let the ambush begin."

On the porch, they listen to Cindy.

"She sounds happy," Kay remarks.

"Let's see how long that lasts."

Kay knocks as the two of them step inside.

From the kitchen, Cindy yells, "Hi, come on in." She steps out of the kitchen, freezing, locking eyes with Kay. "Oh shit, it's you."

"Hi," Kay replies. "Do you remember me?"

"Uh-huh." Cindy eyes drift to Ann. "Are you?" Ann nods. "Shit. You're here about Tom?" They both nod. "Christ."

"Sorry to do this to you," Kay says. Silence. It's awkward.

Cindy smiles. "Ah, it's okay. I think we did the same thing to you."

"The night you showed up with those reporters?"

"Uh-huh."

"Yeah, I guess so? When did Tom have you list this?" Kay asks.

"Yesterday."

"He was here, yesterday?" Ann asks. Cindy nods. "Did he say where he was going?"

"I didn't even think to ask."

"And he gave you a contact number?"

"He did."

"Can I get it?"

"I can't do that. But I can tell him you were here."

"Can you? That would be great."

Cindy calls. "Hi, Tom, some of your friends are here at your house—" She touches her head. "Ahhh, Kay and Ann. Anyway, they wanted me to let you know they're here. Talk to you later."

"Voice mail?" Ann asks. Cindy nods. "Damn."

"He told me he would check in every other day."

"And that works for you?"

"Sure. Bids and offers take time."

"Great, he's going to call you before me," Ann remarks. "What was he like? You know, happy, sad, depressed?"

"Oh, I don't know? Reflective maybe? He wasn't sad or depressed, well, maybe a little depressed. He seems like a guy ready to move on." Ann nods. "He hasn't been in contact?"

"No," Ann replies. Her eyes well up, holding back tears.

"Oh, sorry to hear that." There's an awkward silence. Cindy focuses on Ann. "Do ya mind if I ask a question?"

Ann composes herself. "No, go ahead."

Cindy points at Kay. "That night we were at your place, we left." She points at Ann. "And we went to your place. All these reporters and media people had just been there."

"Yeah."

"I figured out you had two houses, but how did they all figure it out, like at the same time? It's like it was posted or announced to the whole world."

Ann grimaces—she isn't ready for the question. She looks at the floor and then catches Cindy's gaze. "You figured it out?" Cindy nods. "I'm not sure. It surprised me. Boy, that seems like another lifetime."

"Just wondering."

Brett pays the cab driver, turning his attention to the office as he slings the backpack over his shoulder. *This is it, the point of no return.* Breathing in the sea air, he wallows in the smell; he loves the smell of the marina. He limps toward the office door. Pushing open the door, a string of little bells rang, announcing his arrival. Vicky is working at the desk.

Vicky lights up with a big smile. "Brett."

"Hi, Vicky."

"I haven't seen you in a while."

"I've been working a lot lately."

"Ahh. Well, it's good to see you. I have a note here about you." She snatches a post-it note. "You're finally going to do it."

"Yep. I saw it come up for sale, and I couldn't believe my eyes. I guess they call it fate, or something? Anyway, the timing is perfect."

"What happened to your leg?"

"Oh, workin', you know?"

She nods. "This is your big day. Fifty-three thousand. It says here you're paying in cash?"

"Yep."

"You know, we can finance it for you?"

"I know. You know I've been saving for this?"

"Yeah, I know," she remarks. "Okay then, you'll need to sign here, and here. The slip is $239.00 a month. Unless you're moving the boat? The slip is paid up until the end of the month."

"No, this will be my port." After signing, he retrieves the cashier's check from his backpack, placing it on the desk. Vicky inspects the check while Brett counts out two hundred and fifty in cash. She places the key on the desk.

"Here's the key. That sure is a nice boat. Of course, I don't need to tell you that, you've rented the damn thing so many times. We joke around here that it's actually your boat. Hell, the owner never took it out much—My husband was thinking of buying it."

"Really?"

"Yep. He's got this thing in his head about sailing the Caribbean."

"That is the boat to do it in. He's close to retiring, isn't he?"

"Yeah, and once he gets something in his head—Anyway, I'm not sure I want to live on a boat for months at a time. But that's what he wants to do, so I'll probably end up doin' it. Of course, I could just divorce his ass." They laugh.

"Tell George I'm sorry I bought his boat."

"I'm so glad you stepped in. You saved me—You gave me a little time. If he'd had another day to think about it, I'm sure he would have bought it."

Brett smiles. "I didn't have to think about it. It took me exactly three seconds to decide."

"Like I said, we all joke about it being your boat, and now it is."

"That sounds strange when you say it like that. It's going to take a bit to get used to. Okay, thanks, Vicky."

"Enjoy yourself." Vicky nods, smiling. Brett smiles. He nods and limps out of the office.

Brett snakes through the pier to the slip where his new boat is docked; a thirty-nine-foot Cape Horn sailboat. *God, that's a beautiful sight. And now it's mine. Well, Skinny, looks like ya gave me one gift—The balls to get off my ass and buy this beauty.* He climbs aboard. He walks from stern to bow, inspecting. This boat really needs two people to man it. He's sailed it alone, twice. It's not easy, but doable. Under the circumstances, he doesn't have much choice but to sail alone. He unlocks the hatch and goes below, throwing his backpack on one of the chairs. He runs through his checklist, preparing the boat to sail. Back up on deck, wheel at the ready, he fires up the engine. Freeing the boat from the dock, he sets sail for the Gulf of Mexico. He wants to raise the sails, but he's got a schedule to keep, and with the sails up, it would take too long to get to his destination. *God, this is a great way to travel.* He glances at his watch. *Okay, three hours or so, and I should be there.*

Martin and the Rangers are at Eddy's junkyard. They enter an office that hasn't been properly cleaned for at least ten years. Old, dated posters of young women selling auto parts, oil, and tools are pinned to the walls; dates on some of the calendars go back to 1999. Hal works the phone while the officers wait. Hal's hands are as greasy as his shirt, which should have been washed a month ago. The room is filled with fumes of oil and engine cleaner. An impact wrench sings out in the background to complete the mood. Hal hangs up the phone, wiping his hands with a rag before offering it to Martin.

"Sheriff. How the hell are ya?"

"Good. You look busy," Martin remarks.

"Hell, it never stops around here. It's always somethin'. What can I do ya for?"

"We're here about a truck ya guys towed the other night."

"A truck, you say. It wouldn't be the one we towed from Sylvia's, would it?"

"How'd—"

"I figured. I couldn't figure out why the owner wasn't from around here? I wasn't actually there—Gene towed it." Hal presses the button on the intercom. "Hey, Gene, can ya come to the office?" The sound echoes over the yard with a little feedback for ambiance.

"How's the family?" Martin asks.

"That kid of mine is a piece of—"

Gene pops his head in. "Whatcha need Hal?"

"Ah, yeah, these men need to know about that truck ya towed over at Sylvia's."

Gene surveys the room as they nod. He smiles. "It was in the back, ya know, in that clearin' by her barn."

"Say what?" Don remarks.

"Yeah. Brett Hart called it in and said Sylvia wanted it removed. I guess because it was abandoned there, or something like that? I didn't know the truck—it wasn't from around here. I don't know? Brett met me there."

"Wait a second," Martin chimes in. "Brett was there?"

"Yeah. He watched me hook it up."

The officers lock eyes.

"Oh shit," Martin remarks. "Thank you, Hal, Gene." The officers brush by Gene as they rush out the door.

Martin reaches his car, grabbing the mic. "Mel, send someone over to Brett Hart's place. Hold him if he's there. I'm on my way." Martin looks at Jim and Don. "Okay boys, let's roll."

The officers pull up to Brett's house. Mel leans on his car. The Rangers park across the street. Martin pulls his vehicle into Brett's driveway, parking cockeyed. Mel stands up straight. The three men rush him.

"He's not here," Mel says.

"Did ya check his garage?"

"No. But I walked the property. There's no one inside, unlessin' he's hidin' in there. But why would he do that?"

"Oh shoot," Martin says, heading toward the side of the house. The three men follow. Martin stops at the back garage door. A shabby curtain partially covers the garage door window. Martin peeks.

"Shit, his truck's gone. Okay, Mel, get on the horn and let's see if he's around."

"You got it, Sheriff." Mel scoots off.

"Ya think he's headed to the border?" Jim asks.

"I reckon so?"

"Okay, it's been a pleasure, Sheriff. We'll put out an alert statewide on his plate. We'll see if we can track him down," Jim says.

Jim and Don jump into their SUV, calling in a trace on Brett and his truck.

Depressed, Ann is back in bed. The bed has been her comfort too much lately. Hiding under the covers in a fetal position, she blocks out the outside world. She aches. *Am I getting sick? I'm not sick, I'm depressed. I'm heartbroken. Tom, why won't you talk to me?* She's been here before, which is why she stopped looking for a partner. *C'mon girl, you can't wallow in your own self-pity. This isn't good. Ya need to get up. Get out of this bed. Get the hell up. I should, but what's the point? Call somebody, anybody. Lester, call Lester. No, the PI. Yeah, call the PI. Call somebody. Get your ass out of this bed. Oh, I'll do it in a minute.* She falls asleep.

Ann sits atop a horse, soaking in the animal's power. *God, what a feeling. What a beautiful animal.* Together, they trot on a ridge, overlooking the ocean. *How is something this massive so graceful?* A warm breeze blows her hair; it's comforting. She halts the horse, stroking the horse's neck. She combs her fingers through the horse's mane, while watching the waves crash onto the beach. The sunset catches her eye. *What a beautiful sunset. I don't ever remember a sunset this beautiful. God, what a perfect moment.* The beach is calling, seducing her. *It would be great to go down to the beach and ride the horse alongside the waves.* Giving in, she tugs the leather strap to the left, nudging the horse toward the beach. *Wow, I never want to leave.*

Transitioning from the ridge to the sand is tricky. The sand swallows the horse's front legs close to the knee—the horse freezes. Ann kicks the horse. The horse spooks. She pushes, commanding the horse to move forward. The horse rears up. Ann hangs on. The front legs return to the sand, buckling, throwing her face-first into the sand. Like a steam roller, the horse follows, rolling over her, crushing her, forcing her into the sand. She gasps for air. The weight is so extreme. *Oh my God! I'm going to die. He's so heavy.* She's certain her guts are being squeezed out like toothpaste out of a tube. *Help, help, help! Breathe. I can't breathe.* The moment has arrived—her final breath. The horse rolls off, freeing her. Popping her head up, desperate, fighting to breathe but she inhales sand—she coughs. She jerks. Her eyes open. She's awake.

She shakes. *Damn, what was that? Shit.* Tossing the blankets, she sits up. The trauma subsides but the terror of the moment lingers. She folds her arms. *It was a dream. Damn, that seemed so real. Was that because I was buried in my blankets?* Pulling her legs together, she draws her knees up, resting her head, staring at the wall, pondering. *Wow, it was just a dream.* The dream consumes her thoughts. *That seemed so real.* She sighs, dragging her fingers through her hair. She looks at her robe. *Maybe that's my subconscious way of saying get the hell out of bed? That's a helluva way to tell me.*

Slipping into her robe, she grabs her phone, sliding it into her pocket. She wanders the halls like a zombie. *The horse. The beach. Oh yeah, that sunset.* The sunset made an impression. She's on autopilot as she makes coffee. The dream consumes her thoughts. She leans against the counter, arms folded, while the coffee machine throws out a sucking noise. *Lester. Yeah, Lester. Lester knows those psychics. Maybe they can help me decipher it?*

"So, you didn't die?" Lester asks.

"Right."

"How did you feel when you were under the horse?"

"Panic—complete terror—helpless—I couldn't move—I couldn't breathe. I thought I was dead. I had no air left. It felt so real."

"Wow. That doesn't sound fun. Okay, so you thought you were going to die. How did you feel? You know, when you were riding the horse?"

"How did I feel? . . . Huh . . . Powerful. Yeah, powerful."

"Okay, powerful. You're powerful and you were helpless . . . Wait a second, how do you feel with Tom?"

"Tom? Tom . . . Powerful."

"Okay, so we got power. And the sunset?"

"Yeah, that was amazing—so beautiful. I think I'll remember that sunset forever."

"Huh . . . Here's something. Could this be your life with Tom—symbolically?"

Silence. It's like she's been slapped in the face. She chews on this insight a little longer.

"Wow. You know, you're good at this."

"I've been fascinated with dreams since I was a little kid—They're so powerful when you can remember them. Of course, some are more important than others. This one is important—a message dream."

"It's certainly got my attention. It felt so real."

"You thought you were going to die?"

"I was sure of it. The weight of the horse—I thought my guts were going to be squeezed out on the beach. But it only left me wounded."

"Like you are now?" Silence. There's a long pause. "I think I hit a nerve?"

"Yeah," Ann replies, softly. "Damn . . . I think you're on to something. It sure scared the hell out of me."

"I can see that."

"Maybe it's time to move on from him? Shit, I shouldn't be telling you this."

"It's okay. This is between you and me," Lester remarks.

"Anything? Have you heard anything?"

"No, he still hasn't popped up. What about the PI? Have you heard from him?"

"No, nothing."

"Sorry."

"Thanks for helping me process the dream."

"You got it."

Ann stares off, pondering their conversation. The dream haunts her. *I need to stop this. I should go somewhere and get out of the house. A trip, maybe, I should take a trip? It's time to move on. Damn, I thought he was the one. Damn, damn, damn.* She calls Kay.

"Hi, girlfriend," Kay says.

"Hi."

"This is a switch."

"What's that?"

"You're calling me."

Ann chuckles. "I call you."

"Yeah, but not much."

"Hey, have you got any time off?"

"A little, I think. What's up?"

"How would you like to take a trip?"

"Ya serious?"

"Yeah, I need to get out of here. Wallowing in my own pity is so depressing. But I don't think I should travel alone—"

"Is this going to be in Ann style?"

"What's that mean?"

"You know, private jet and limos?"

Ann laughs. "Yep. Ann style."

"When do we leave? Wait, where are we going?"

"I haven't figured that one out yet."

"Oh shoot."

"What?"

"I do need to check to see if I have any time left. Let me see what I can work out at work."

Jim pursues the report. Don drives. Jim looks up.

"Well?" Don asks.

"I don't know? Maybe he got across the border before we put out the alert?"

"Bus, what about the bus?"

"I looked. Nothing." The computer beeps.

"Oh okay, we got something." Jim reads. "His truck, it's got a new owner; the registration has just been updated."

"Did he sell his truck?"

"Maybe, it's a dealer—not a private party."

"I'll be damned," Don remarks. "This boy is gone. Looks like we're in pursuit of a slick one. He got a helluva jump on us if he's already made it across the border. Okay, where are we headed?"

"Let's see, looks like 2700 East Price Road."

The Rangers pull up at M&H Auto. They shoulder up as they approach the main office. Phil gets up to greet them at the door.

"Oh crap, did we buy a stolen vehicle?" Phil fires off.

"Howdy," Don says. Phil nods.

"No, at least I don't think so," Jim remarks.

"Whew. How ya boys doing today?" Phil asks.

"Good," the Rangers reply.

"We're looking into the Ford F-150 you just registered—"

"Yep, I knew it. There was something not right about that one. I could feel it in my bones."

"You know the truck we're talking about."

"Yeah, yeah. A young fella—he walked with a limp."

"He had a limp?"

"Yeah. Seemed like a nice fella, but isn't that what they say about serial killers?"

"Yeah, I guess they do?"

"He sold his truck—how much did he get?" Don asks.

"I don't know if I can say? Can I do that?"

"We can get a warrant and pull the record."

"Oh hell, seventy-five hundred. He asked for it in cash."

"Cash." Don and Jim share a glance. "Was someone with him?"

"Nah, he was alone. He had a cab pick him up. Looked like he had it all set up?"

"How do ya know that?"

"The cab was waiting."

"Do you remember the cab company?"

"Ya know—I don't—wait a second, Valley. Yeah, Valley Cab. Ya don't see that one around here much."

"Anything else?"

"Not really. Like I said, he walked with a limp."

Brett sails into the Port of El Mezquital, Mexico. It's a quiet, small fishing village; he's been coming here for months. He's made a few friends and the Port Authority knows him; it's easy for him to get in and out. He even has a special place to dock. He glances at his watch. *Okay, the bus should have arrived in San Fernando an hour and a half ago.* A helpful young man, Juan, helps him dock the boat.

"Hola, Señor Brett."

"Hola, Juan. Como has estado?"

"Muy bien."

With the boat secure, he steps on the dock, shaking the cramps. His leg is stiff. After working the leg for about fifty feet, it loosens up. *Seems like it's getting better. Or is that my imagination?*

He asks Juan if he's hungry, which he is. Brett takes him down the street to a place he found many months ago that serves fresh seafood. They chat. Brett inquiries about Juan's uncle; he flies a mail plane to San Fernando; it's a short plane ride. Juan makes a call. His uncle agrees to take him, but he's about to make his run for the day, so they need to hurry. His uncle and the airfield are across the bay.

Juan shuttles him across the bay in his small runabout boat. A truck is waiting to take Brett to the airfield.

Juan's uncle, Carlos, is a kind man. He wouldn't take money from Brett, saying this is his normal route and Brett was a rider. The plane is a little four-seat Cessna. The flight took twenty-five minutes, and the landing was the best Brett could ever remember. The best part: he is at the San Fernando Airport. Brett has a half-hour before the return flight—perfect.

Inside, Brett stops at the departure board. *I hope the flight hasn't been canceled.* The flight is still running. *Sweet.* Waiting in a short line, he works his way up to the counter.

"Hola."

"Hola. Quiero un billete a Guadalajara."

The agent smiles, tapping the keyboard. "Quiero facturar una maleta?"

"No, I have the one bag."

"Oh, you speak English, sir?" Brett nods. "Okay then. I will need your passport."

Here's the decisive moment. Brett shakes. *Shit man, calm down.* The agent has a curious look as Brett slides his passport. There are these moments in life where you sense something is off, not right. This is that moment for the agent. The agent pauses, looking at the passport. He pushes past the internal red flags and bangs away on the keyboard. The agent pauses. Brett feels his heartbeat. This is some intense shit. Sweat collects on his brow—armpits. Brett tugs his collar. His eyes dart, looking, searching for an escape route—in case one is needed. The agent gives a slight smile. Brett smiles back. They wait. *Fuck, this is taking too long. What the fuck is the hold-up?* The agent locks eyes with Brett.

The agent dips his head and speaks in a low voice, "This is so strange . . . It says you are wanted in Texas."

Crap, shit fuck! Caught. Run. Do it now, run! Slowly swiveling his head, he spots a gap in the line behind him. An old lady drops her purse; she's scrambling to collect her belongings. She's creating a distraction. *I think I can dart between that lady* —. A jolt—an insight. A calm feeling overtakes him—*this is Mexico.* Brett squares up with the counter. "It does?"

"Yes, sir," The agent eyes the law enforcement officer, standing by the main door.

Brett has a small amount of cash in his hand. Pulling up his backpack, he fumbles through the pocket with money. He pulls out a fistful. Counting out $400, he places it on the counter.

Brett, in a low voice, "Are you sure?" The agent tilts his head, glancing at the cop. Brett counts out another $200, adding it to the pile. The agent narrows his eyes, glancing at the people in line, behind Brett. Brett counts another $200, adding it to the pile.

In a full voice, "Huh, I don't know what happened," the agent remarks, scooping up the money. "Would you like a window seat?"

"Si."

"That will be 2,8853.02 pesos."

"How much is that in dollars?"

"One hundred forty-four dollars." Brett smiles, paying the man. If anything could have caused Brett to have a heart attack, this is it. *Damn, I need a drink.* He stows the ticket in his backpack. He breathes. *Okay, that's done. Now, can I get my ass out of Mexico?*

Brett walks up to Carlos' plane, he's refueling. Brett tries to give him money—he refuses. Brett gets a strange vision: He sees Mexican police storming the tarmac, shooting, taking him into custody. He shakes the thought. Looking at the tarmac, all is calm.

Loaded up in the plane, Carlos runs through his checks, and they're back in the air. It is a pleasant plane ride back.

A short trip across the bay, and he's back in town. Making a trip to the local market, he stocks up for the next leg of his journey. Juan finishes topping his fuel tank. He slides Juan an extra hundred, encouraging him to give some to his uncle. Juan helps him disembark from the pier. They wave. Making his way back out to the Gulf of Mexico, he drifts, reviewing the scene at the ticket counter. *Man, that was dumb. Why didn't I just sail away? Of course, if this works, they will be chasing a ghost.* Speaking of ghosts, a vision of Skinny creeps in.

He's back at Sylvia's barn, standing with the bat at the ready, waiting for Skinny to bolt out of the barn—crack. *It must have been the adrenaline, I really hit him hard.* He sweats. His heartbeat races. His thoughts jump to his family. *Man, I won't be able to see them anymore. Even if I could, how could I look them in the eye, knowing what I did? Some of them would be happy, thinking I was a hero. But still, he was family.* Visions of Skinny wielding the ice pick intrude; he jerks. *Is this shit going to haunt me for the rest of my life? Maybe it should.*

He kills the motor, releasing the sails. It takes a second for the wind fill the sails—snap, the sails become full. He monitors the gauges, setting the autopilot. For the first time, in a long time, he kicks back, relaxing. He basks in the sun as the wind washes over his face. *Damn, this is fucking great.* He checks his wounds. The leg is almost healed. The arm has a way to go. Skinny invades his thoughts. *Man, I thought taking out that motherfucker would bring more relief.* Skinny is dead, but he lives on his head. *Why am I still afraid of that motherfucker? I need an exorcism.*

For the moment, he flushes thoughts of Skinny by focusing on what's next. *What will it be? Fishing, charter boat, scooters? Maybe I can work in a bar? Man, I'm glad I learned Spanish. That can come in handy.* Plan A was to go to Cancun or Playa del Carmen, but now that he's wanted, it's on to plan B. *I can't do Mexico now. I guess that's one good thing about the shit that went down at the airport. I don't have to guess anymore. Better I know now.* He sets a course for Cuba.

Don and Jim sit in their SUV.

"Okay, where's Valley Cab?" Don asks.

"Hang on a second. Here it is. 147 Palm Boulevard."

They pull up to 147 Palm Boulevard, which is a tiny strip mall. The Valley Cab's office is sandwiched between an Auto Insurance company and a Latino barber shop—there are five parking slots—all of them taken. It's a boulevard, so there's no parking on the street.

"Hell, park on the side street. Let's walk in," Jim says.

They're attracting attention; you never see the Texas Rangers in this part of town. As they reach the door of Valley Cab, three Latino males scramble out of the barber shop, jumping in their cars, racing off.

"Look at that—three spots just became available. I guess we didn't wait long enough?" They laugh.

"And they seem to be in a damn hurry," Jim remarks.

"A special at a department store? Hey, maybe they were called home for dinner?" They laugh.

"It's a little early for dinner—don't ya think?"

"Yeah, I guess?"

Inside Valley Cab, a young heavyset woman is on the phone, smoking. Don notices that her ashtray is overflowing. A voice booms from the back.

"How can I help you, gentleman?" A middle-aged, balding man steps into view with a wrinkled shirt, a cigarette hangs from his lips.

"Hi. We need information on a rider," Don says.

Under his breath, Jim mumbles, "Jesus, does everyone smoke in this place?"

He waves. "Come on back." The Rangers work their way to his office, passing a water cooler and a few empty desks. The place is a mess. Entering the man's office, files and papers are stacked on the desk and tables, even on the floor. Jim and Don stand in front of the man's desk. "Hi, so what cab was it?"

"Not sure, but the rider was picked up at M&H Auto," Don says.

"Do you know the address?"

"It's on Price Road," Jim says.

He scrolls through a log on the computer.

"Ah, here it is. Let's see, Skinny was the driver—"

"You're shitting me?" Don says.

"Really, Skinny?" Jim asks.

"You two know Skinny?"

"No, but if ya knew the background—ah, never mind," Jim says.

"Is Skinny in trouble? Did he do something?"

"No, no. He's fine."

"Skinny has been with me the longest. So, ya don't know Skinny?"

"It's an interesting name, that's all," Don says.

The man returns to working the computer.

"Okay, it looks like he took 'em to the bus terminal."

"Okay, thanks."

"Anything else?"

"No. Thank you."

"That's it?"

"Yep. That's it. Thank you for your help."

The Rangers sit in the SUV, staring.

"Now what?" Don asks.

"We had this before."

"I know. We charge him with murder, they won't extradite him."

"If we say he's a person of interest, they won't extradite him. You think the Sheriff back in Sterling City has charged him?"

"I don't see anything."

"Has he popped up on the grid?"

"Let's see." Jim pops on the US immigration portal. "Okay, he bought a bus ticket to San Fernando. Oh shit—"

"What?"

"He bought an airline ticket from San Fernando to Guadalajara." Don looks at his watch. "How did he do that? I get the bus ticket but buying the plane ticket . . . they should have nabbed him."

"It's Mexico."

"I guess."

"You up for some Mexican food?"

"Sure. At least we got where he went, but once he lands, he could be anywhere."

"He is headed to the Southwest of Mexico."

"True. We got one thing going for us."

They say it together, "A white guy with a limp."

Ann sips her coffee; she's waiting for Kay's call. Antsy, she picks up a book. She's not reading. She daydreaming. *Maybe, TV.* She scrolls through the guide, but nothing grabs her. Turning off the TV, she sighs. *Damn, Kay, when ya going to call girl.* She's back in the kitchen, picking up the newspaper. She's not reading—not really. Her eyes are looking at the paper and scanning the words, but she's daydreaming. Her thoughts bounce on mundane things, like when does the gardener come next? Why is Kay taking so long to call. *She seemed excited to go, didn't she? Yeah, she did.* She gazes at her watch.

The dream intrudes; the sunset, horse, being crushed. She lowers the paper, staring at the couch. The couch. Yes, that couch. The place where they first made love. *God, that was amazing.* Her body quivers. *Where are you, Thomas? No, I have to move on. It's time. Yeah, it's time. The dream made that clear. How can I do that? Jesus, Thomas, you're like heroin.* Every place she looks reminds her of him. *Jesus, this is like living with the memory of a dead person. How is that possible? He wasn't even here that long. I think I'm going to need to sell this place.* Her eyes sweep the kitchen and living room. *Yeah, this place is nice. I do love this place. But I can get another one just as nice, maybe nicer. I like the idea of that. Yeah, something nicer. That's the answer—I'll sell this place. If I'm going to make a break, it needs to be clean. Yeah. That feels better. God, I can't believe how much better I feel.*

She leans against the counter, arms folded, staring out. *Interesting how making a decision helps. Isn't that what Tom said? Choices are not good or bad, and I need this. If I'm going to move on, I need this. Why hasn't Kay called?* She stares at her phone. *Where are you, girlfriend? I know she still works and all, but we have places to go. I need to get out of this house. Damn, girl, why haven't you called? Maybe I should call her?* Her phone rings. *Finally.* She does a double-take—it's Tom. She answers but doesn't speak.

"Hello." Tom peeks at the number, checking. "Hello. Ann. Are you there?"

"I'm here . . . Tell me you're dying."

"No, I'm not dying."

"You lost your phone?"

"Look, I know what I did was shitty."

"Ya, think? What the hell?"

"I don't know—I needed to work some things out. I've been in a dark place."

"You're not alone on that one, Kemo Sabe." Silence. "Tom, this has been hell."

"I know, I know, I'm sorry. I literally turned off my phone."

"After all we've been through together? You couldn't give me one little call?"

"I didn't want to be tracked, so I turned off my phone."

"Well, it worked. Not even my PI could find you. Where are you?"

"I'm at the Carlton in St. Thomas."

"Hold it, you're in St. Thomas? At the Carlton? The Ritz-Carlton?"

"You're right. This place is spectacular."

"Isn't that rich? Thomas in St. Thomas."

"I've hadn't thought of it that way. I'm looking at the ocean right now."

"Great—I've been in hell and you're looking at a beach. Shit. Well, I guess you're a learn fast."

"Ann."

"Yes."

"I miss you."

"You do?"

"I do."

"But you haven't called. You ghosted me."

"No, no, I didn't ghost you. It's just that I've been working through some things. I know what I did was pretty shitty. Ann . . . I miss you. Really, I miss you." Silence. Tom is not sure what to say. "Are you still there?"

"I'm here." More silence. "Our foundation is built on sand."

"Sand? What sand? What are you talking about?"

"You wouldn't understand. You should understand, but you don't."

"You're right. What are you talking about?"

"It was a dream I had."

"A dream?"

"Yeah."

"Maybe, I should call later."

"You can't do this to me."

"Do what?"

"Call up, out of the blue—"

"I think my timing is bad. I'll call later. I love you." Click.

Ann listens to the dial tone. "Bye." She drops the phone on the counter. *You fucking asshole. You call up, out of the blue, and tell me you miss me? What, I'm your on-call girlfriend? Is that it? You asshole. The nerve. Shit. I liked it better when I didn't know where you were.* Ann stares at her phone. She paces.

What am I, a convenience? Something he can pull off the shelf when he feels like it? A toy? Who the hell does he think he is? She stops with an insight. *Of course, he has been through a lot. But that's no excuse for not telling me what's going on. Oh shit, unless he was thinking of ending things? He did say he was in a dark place. Or worse, ending himself? Oh shit. What if that's what was going on? Damn. C'mon Ann, you can be rough on people—you know this. Kay tells me that a lot. Yeah, I am. But he could've called. Why was that such a chore for him? One little call—what's so damn hard about that? Not wanting to be tracked—what kind of BS is that? What about the dream? I can't be with him. C'mon Ann, are you going to let a stupid little dream run your life? But our foundation is built on sand. Damn, my track record with other people sucks. I push them away. Is that what I'm doing? Damn, that's so true, I push them away.* She paces. *I should call Kay. No, I'm a big girl. I can figure this out.* She stops, looking at the couch. She sits on the couch in that spot—the place where it all started. She closes her eyes, soaking it in. She's transported back to that moment—she can feel Tom. It all floods back; the explosion, the ecstasy. Their skin touching. Her senses are heightened. Her breathing is heavy. Her eyes open. *Damn, I was ready to move on. At least I was playing with the idea of moving on. I could search for the rest of my days on this planet, and no one could live up to Tom. He's ruined me. Shit, I'm ruined. You ruined me, Thomas. Are you going to let a dream stop that?* She runs to the counter, grabbing her phone.

"Hi, I need a plane to St. Thomas . . ."